Route 52

By Gerry Foster

Copyright ©2025 Gerry Foster
All rights reserved

Cover design and graphics
by Ragley Road Studios

ISBN: 9798265703118

Dedication

To Dave, who has supported this work
with editing, presentation and graphics

To all my friends and family

To bus drivers everywhere…

With thanks and appreciation to
W.J. Featherstone,
Joan Banting and Joan Khurody
for their encouragement and advice

A percentage of the sales from this book
will go to Cancer Research UK

All characters in this book are fictitious,
inspired by those met on life's journey…

You can become absorbed in people-watching, when you're on a park bench, at the seaside, in a café or from a bus. When it's getting dark, you can snatch a sneaky peak into the windows of the houses you pass, before the curtains are closed and anyone realises you've caught their moment.

Looking around you on the bus is intriguing. Where are the people going? It may seem obvious, as you observe school uniform, shopping trolleys, child in the buggy, but the truth may be so different.

It was the No 52 bus, on such ordinary Wednesdays. Although the windows were invariably grimy, no one was apparently bothered about trying to see out. They just seemed to know where they were… and where they were going.

There was the repetitive screeching of brakes as the doors opened and banged shut, people talking, faint background noise escaping from earphones and the bell ringing as people signalled the driver to stop. People on the pavement stood aside, not noticing who was pushing past on to the street, intent as they were on getting aboard themselves.

We often speak of journeying together. On a regular bus journey we're an unusual group of companions, creating an unusual kind of family, with unusual stories…

Chapter 1
A real-life detective story

She was 18 years old, sitting apart from the others in the same uniform. They giggled and laughed out loud glancing in her direction. She wore earphones and kept her eyes fixed on the grimy window. Only one more stop on this No 52 bus.

The bell rang, but she took her time picking up her stuff and kept her head down, thanking the driver, while they all got off and turned in the direction of school. They'd already lost interest in her, so didn't notice, as she moved off amongst the waiting passengers on the kerb, taking the opposite direction. Bullying and all kind of abuse would now be a thing of the past, she thought, with a mixture of relief and triumph.

Gemma disappeared round a corner and considered…this was it…She would do just that…disappear. After every shift at the superstore, she'd calculated how much she'd saved. At last, this day had finally arrived

It had taken all her inner strength and that overused word 'resilience' to work as hard as she could, in a world of her own at school and at home, keeping herself going, as she ticked off the days. No one guessed that her last exam was yesterday, as today she'd got up and gone out as usual, dressed for school. No one would have noticed the larger than usual backpack containing all the personal things she could fit inside. She'd written her notice at the required time and received an email giving a glowing reference for any other of the superstore's branches. She'd handed into school all her books. At home, no one would come in her tidy bedroom. Her mother and partner had left in the early hours that day for their holiday, with neither a word, nor a backward glance. When they returned in two weeks, they would quite simply find she'd gone.

What's the difference between feeling fear, anxiety and excitement? Gemma had planned every detail. She wondered if the person intent on committing the perfect crime felt like this. She felt happy she was now legally an adult and wasn't breaking any law.

Slipping into the public toilets, Gemma changed into the most unobtrusive outfit and stuffed her uniform in a bag at the bottom of the bin, covering it with paper towels. She only felt relief to get rid of it. Gemma looked round to ensure she'd left nothing behind. Her belt bag was now safely under her jacket, with all her essential documents double checked.

Gemma had noted down carefully all the stages of the route on her phone. She felt hungry and found a bench on the station platform to eat the lunch she'd packed while she waited for the first of her train connections. Then finally she reached the airport. Gemma once more checked all was safely in her belt bag. Passport, purse, phone. Not that she needed her passport for the Isle of Man, but she wanted all her important documents safely with her.

She thought back to the shock of an earlier conversation, when out of the blue Luke had declared, "I've got something to tell you. I'm so mad about it all – we're moving!" Gemma had listened, her mind in a whirl. Moving? Where? Why? When?

* * *

Luke's mother, Lin, worked in finance and his father, Chris, in education. They'd both secured promotional jobs and the

Isle of Man was in his mother's blood. She was Manx. They were moving back. Luke had enjoyed some wet and windy holidays there growing up and liked the water sports. Luke wanted to become a personal trainer. Yes, it seemed openings and opportunities were over there, but it was so far away from Gemma. What about their plans? He was two years older than her, but they absolutely knew they wanted to stay together.

Gemma and Luke had thought it through, and email exchanges had yo-yoed back and forth. Gemma had been concerned at first that Luke would just find another girlfriend, a soulmate. But he'd insisted a deal with his parents was on. As they were going to be financially better off on the Isle of Man, they would help him with a place of his own to rent. When Gemma could leave home, they'd live together.

Gemma really liked Luke's parents. They took a real interest in him. Yes, there had been some 'discussion' about their plans, but she was so relieved there was an agreement. They had found a flat and all the legalities had been done through a solicitor. Gemma had been included in a couple of holidays over the last few years. She thought they probably felt sorry for her… but maybe they liked her as well. They'd known things weren't good at her home, especially after her mother's new partner actually moved in. Gemma had loved being by the sea, whatever the blustery weather on the Isle of Man. She felt reinvigorated and so much happier. She had decided with Luke's agreement to write to his parents, explaining that she'd done everything she possibly could to prepare for this move, waiting till she'd finished her 'A' levels etc. She had an excellent reference and intended to start by finding a job in one of the superstores. Fortunately, the chain had just opened a couple of branches on the island, with more promised. Gemma omitted to say that she wasn't telling anyone else what she was doing. That could work itself out. She hoped Luke's parents would be happy for her to be there with Luke.

Her heart pounded, as the escalator brought her to the Manx airlines check in. Doubts began to crowd her mind and for a moment she felt sick. Deep breaths, she told herself in the departure lounge. There was time for a quick change in the toilets. Gemma carefully exchanged her nondescript top for the one she'd found in the charity shop. It looked like it had never been worn. The original label was still on it anyway, so she'd decided to buy just this one thing. Hoodie down, hair brushed and a final check. Nothing was left behind. Then the call to board and she was on the airplane. Breathe…

There was the alert to turn off mobile phones or switch to flight mode, but firstly 'ping' in came the missed call text. She checked for messages…none left.

Her chest tightened…was everything OK?

* * *

The plane landed. All the passengers went to baggage retrieval and straight out into the foyer of Ronaldsway airport, while Gemma just made her way to the door, searching for Luke. No one. Gemma checked her phone. Nothing. She rang Luke again. No pickup.

People were being met and drove off. She was the only one, left on her own. Her mind raced. The only thing to do was to make her way to the flat, but then Luke's parents' new home was closer. She knew where it was, so maybe it would make more sense to go there. Perhaps they'd heard from Luke. There must be a simple explanation.

It was only a short walk to Lin and Chris's house from the bus stop. Gemma was flabbergasted. It was huge. House prices made all the difference she assumed. You could obviously get more 'bang for your buck' here.

Nervously Gemma approached the door and put on as carefree a face as possible.

No one answered. Gemma felt her heart skip. She tried ringing Luke again. Still no reply. She sent a text to Luke to let him know where she was.

Should she go round to the back of the house? Really, this was stupid. She was acting like she was in a detective drama. She peeped through the letterbox, but it was impossible to see anything much, so she made her way through the side gate. Considering they'd only lived there a few months, the garden was a picture – Gemma guessed this must have been the perfect place to move straight into.

Feeling like she was invading their privacy, Gemma nevertheless peered through the windows, noting a sitting room and office. What a place this was for two or three people! Checking the time, she realised they could both still be at work. She returned to the front of the house through the side gate, securing it behind her.

Gemma noticed that the side of the front garden dropped down to the river and she could just make out a jetty where a boat was moored. Gemma wandered down and then looked back up at the house. From this standpoint, she could also take in a summerhouse and two double garages. This was a huge step up on their home in the UK.

Just then the sound of a vehicle approaching the drive prompted Gemma to get out of sight. She felt ridiculously guilty. Gemma decided to be sensible, after all, what was the point in skulking down here when it could be Lin or Chris or even Luke who'd arrived.

A blue Skoda, which reminded of her late father's car arrived. That make of car had been mocked for years but then it seemed to take on a new popularity, so her father had felt vindicated in buying one. Gemma's heart skipped and a sense of foreboding hit the base of her stomach, as she saw two men pause at the door, look round the outside of the house as she had done and then after pausing again, enter the house. What was happening? But in minutes, they exited looking round, clutching boxes, before they sped off. She didn't know what made her do it, just instinctively, having a good view of the numberplate, she quickly noted it on her phone.

Gemma nervously approached the front door again. It remained closed, but when she now looked through the window, she was shocked that in such a short space of time the office had been turned over. Whoever they were, they were looking for something.

Gemma trembled. This day was just turning into a nightmare. She rang the police. At last, a call from Luke.

* * *

"I'm so sorry, Gemma. I tried to ring earlier to wish you a good flight but lost all signal. Dad's in a state – he doesn't know where Mum is – they were meeting up in town. Your text said you were at Mum and Dad's house?" Luke's call alarmed her, especially when she explained what had happened.

Luke incredulously asked, "Gemma, are you OK? I'm coming right over with Dad!"

In the Isle of Man, distances can't be covered quickly, because there is very little dual carriageway. Luke and his dad arrived to find a police car already outside. The study had indeed been turned over. "Please stay outside. Nothing is to be disturbed," an officer instructed. Luke's eyes scanned the room. It resembled a crime scene in a TV drama. "Dad? What's going on? Where on earth is Mum?" Chris ran his fingers through his hair. "Dad?" questioned Luke again. Chris didn't look up, but his brow was furrowed as he muttered, "There are things that I'm not sure of, that have been happening…" Luke heard his own raised voice as he looked at his dad. "What things? You've only been here a few months, what's gone wrong?" But Chris could only cry back, "I don't know, I don't know!"

After Gemma had been questioned by a police officer, Luke grabbed and hugged her. "Are you OK, Gemma? You saw what happened?" Gemma explained everything to Luke, hoping she'd been able to describe the men, the vehicle and the number plate of the blue Skoda well enough to give a good lead. This was far from the romantic reunion Gemma had hoped for, but she was so relieved and pleased that she and Luke were now together.

An officer approached them. "It would be better if you would all accompany us to the station to make statements." Luke felt sick. This wasn't real. Where was his mum?

On arriving at the police station, Chris was taken away and both Luke and Gemma sensed there was no warm concern in the officer's tone, when he led them into a room to wait.

"What's happening? Where's my Dad? Can we see him?" Luke pleaded.

"Another officer will be with you shortly," was the curt reply.

The officer entered and sat down opposite Luke and Gemma, who sat up straight automatically, as though they were in the headteacher's office. Statements were made and other details noted. Gemma was thankful she had her passport handy, which was checked. Unable to wait any longer, Luke desperately asked, "Please tell me, what's going on? Why have you taken Dad? Do you know where Mum is?"

"All I can tell you at present is that your dad is helping us with enquiries into some financial inconsistencies. We don't know where your mum is and she's not answering her phone, so we're trying to locate her. Do you know anywhere she could be?"

Financial inconsistencies? What does that mean? Luke's mouth was dry. "Please can we have a glass of water?" While the officer left, Luke looked at Gemma and muttered, "I'm just so sorry, Gemma. This wasn't how it was meant to be, after all our planning. Are you OK?" Looking into Luke's eyes, she squeezed his hand and reassured him that everything would be OK, and they'd be here together to do whatever they could. There must have been some sort of mistake. You heard about 'mistaken identity' all the time. Somehow that had to be it.

Carrying a tray with disposable, biodegradable cups of tepid water, the officer returned. Determined to be as helpful as possible, so this could all end, Luke listed the few people he could think of that his mum knew on the Island, who might know where she was. He couldn't speak for work colleagues, but assumed his dad would help with those contacts. He listed familiar places they had returned to for visits for their favourite holiday haunts. 'Haunt' took on another meaning, but he dismissed it. Then Luke remembered his mum had a key to his flat and maybe she'd gone there, but he decided to hold back that information. He wanted to take Gemma there first and if his mum was there, well, they'd cross that bridge when they came to it and give her time to explain.

"Can we see Dad?" Luke pleaded.

"I'm sorry, no," was the officer's formal response. "He needs to remain here for now. You can go, but please don't leave the Island. We'll keep in touch." "Please tell Dad we're here for him!" Luke exclaimed. With that, the officer showed them out. This was ridiculous... "Please don't leave the Island" sounded like some sort of espionage, or other criminal activity was being investigated. "Come on, Gemma, let's go home to our flat!"

* * *

To the rear of the building was a tight parking area, with just space for two vehicles, one behind the other. It was surrounded by walls of the tall seaside houses, converted into flats. There were no overlooking windows. At the far end was Luke's mum's car.

Luke and Gemma exchanged looks – were they worried or relieved? On entering the front door, Luke called out, but there was silence. Slipped beneath a vase of flowers on the table was a note from Lin. "Luke, I'm in a fix. I don't want you to be too. I found something out and now someone's trying to get hold of it. Dad doesn't know anything. I just need to disappear for a bit to think." Then she'd added, "I put your Gemma on the car insurance, so she can have my car." Alongside the note was Lin's mobile phone with lots of missed calls from Chris.

What had she been thinking of…that she was some kind of sleuth? Before leaving her last branch, Lin started having some concerns. It wasn't long after her arrival in the Isle of Man's branch of 'Maximize Your Accounting', that she feared her worries about financial inconsistencies were founded. But were there really inconsistencies or was it just her? This was an Island with a different legal system, government, even banknotes. There must be processes which she needed to get her head round and then it would all make sense. But as the weeks progressed, she felt increasingly worried. It felt significant that she wasn't sure who to take into her confidence. Everyone had been there much longer than her and she realised that although she was Manx, she'd never even worked on the Island before and that put her at a disadvantage. Lin also for the first time felt aware of a gender divide. Even though she had been promoted in taking up this position, she sometimes felt treated like a junior. She had just tried to let it wash over her, determined to get as much experience as possible, but the feeling nagged at her. She couldn't bear to think she had made a mistake in bringing them here, as Chris was already well settled in the Department of Education, Sport and Culture.

It was on a Friday that she stumbled on some client papers revealing figures which gave her a horrible foreboding. Lin thought about what to do. She decided to send a couple of emails, so she had something in writing. This way she hoped to check out a few details with one or two colleagues, as a general enquiry. No one picked up till the Monday, by which time she had regretted what she'd written. Emails could so easily be misunderstood, but working mostly from home, there weren't the casual office conversations to be had. What should she do? She decided to make a call. The colleague was frosty when she attempted to bring the email to his attention. She asked if she could meet up to go over some figures. He said that wouldn't be necessary. Lin explained how she felt it was relevant to the accounts she was dealing with to just check this out. Would he like her to speak to someone else? Again, he said that wouldn't be necessary and that he had to go.

Lin was left feeling upset and very uneasy. As days went on, she felt vulnerable. On impulse on this particular Wednesday, she'd unplugged her laptop, grabbed her phone and with them threw some clothes in a bag, before driving to Luke and Gemma's flat. After a few minutes, from there she had hurriedly walked away.

Luke and Gemma rang the police, to tell them what they'd found. They were really concerned for her safety. Any information could only help to find Luke's mum and to remove his dad from any suspicion. They instinctively didn't touch anything else and waited for the police to arrive.

* * *

The information Gemma was able to give to the police was just the lead the police had been waiting for, in a financial scandal taking up considerable resource for months. Being able to track the blue Skoda so swiftly was an incredible piece of luck. The men they caught were brought in for questioning and the car contents revealed all sorts of useful information for the police enquiry. On questioning Chris, it became clear to the police that he didn't have any idea what Lin had got herself into, but her instincts and experience had proved to be correct. The case would need some unravelling, but there was evidence and there were vital leads to follow up.

The financial inconsistencies Lin had noticed were costing the high-profile businesspeople in the UK millions of pounds, while certain individuals on the Island were able to invest fraudulently overseas tax-free, through their connections. No one had bargained for a woman accountant to be so perceptive. But where was she?

The police were looking through all the CCTV footage available, but they couldn't find her. It was the mobile she'd bought so that she could ring Chris, which helped them to locate her.

Chris called Lin, crying with relief. "I've been out of my mind!"

"I'm so sorry," Lin cried, "but I couldn't risk you getting involved – I just wasn't sure – I must go."

"No, it's OK, the police are on to this. You must come into the station, where I am now to make a statement!"

"What, where are Luke and Gemma?"

"They are at their flat. It's all going to be OK. You don't realise what a brilliant piece of work you've done!"

Not long afterwards, Chris and Lin were meeting together, firstly at the police station to make statements and later at Luke and Gemma's flat. They would need to stay there for now, while their house was, unbelievably, called a 'crime scene' and until others, in addition to the two men involved, had been brought in for questioning. Lin and Chris knew they would be part of the ongoing investigation, but they were reassured that a police presence would remain easily accessible to them. They were amazed at how quick-thinking Gemma had been, as they sat and talked together. Honestly, what were the odds that things could have turned out like this? They chatted on and now they discovered the bit Gemma felt ready to explain, about how difficult her life had become at home. They couldn't believe what a day she had experienced since she caught the No 52 bus that morning and nor could she, as she recalled her earlier thoughts. Unbelievably, it had turned out that she was in a real-life detective story...

Chapter 2
Time to go home

"That sounds like a dog," was often the reply when asked his name. But Rory was so 'over that', to use the expression of his teenage grandson.

"Where are you off to today? Oh of course, it's Wednesday!" Of course, life had its familiar, predictable, old pattern. At least everyone knew where everyone else was going, well, usually…This was the day he later fetched his youngest grandchild from school and was at home for the older ones, so they wouldn't be 'latchkey kids'. Was that expression still used?

Rory tried hard to keep up with the latest turns of phrase, but, if truth be told, by the time he'd caught up, what he said was obviously so 'passé'!

But this was no ordinary Wednesday for Rory. He left the house having checked his list. He had taught himself the importance of lists. Maggie would have laughed out loud, if she were alive. "You just need to keep a list!" she'd declared with an edge of frustration. "You then have the satisfaction of crossing off what you've done!" Rory found that the satisfaction of crossing off on the list, was actually because otherwise he'd forget if he'd done something at all. Checklist sorted and returned to his 'manbag'…who'd have thought it? He used to carry a briefcase.

Rory had plenty of time, but he made his way to the bus stop for the No 52. His grandsons caught the earlier bus to avoid the 'annoying others' who travelled later. But he didn't mind. There was something about feeling a crush of other people around, that reminded you were really alive in the 'here and now'.

The windows were so grimy that Rory couldn't make out where he was, but fortunately the digital cueing was working and he could read which was the next stop. He reassured himself that he always got off after the schoolchildren. It was quiet for a minute when the rabble had left, but more than a usual number of people pressed on to the bus and he felt a moment of panic about reaching the bell and pushing through, but he managed it. His stop. He thanked the driver as always. "Mind how you go, sir!" the driver smiled and, raising a wave, Rory was off the bus. He waited for a moment to look at the list. Which way?

The family joked about his forgetfulness, but, as far as he knew, put it down to his age of 84 years. "Oh, you'll go on for ever!" his daughter regularly exclaimed, while Rory thought…I hope not…

Rory recognised the buildings in general, but not the solicitor's, until he rounded the corner. Time check and list check…all OK so far. He reminded himself of the name of the solicitor for his appointment…Mr Hammond of Hammond & Jessops.

"Good morning, Mr Adams. I understand you've come about your will?" Rory considered. "Yes, I have. I want to rewrite it."

As of September, his three grandsons would be in senior school, the eldest being sixteen and Rory thought him quite old enough to take responsibility both for himself and his brothers. So, Rory was going to leave the town and do what he and Maggie had always planned…take himself back to where they had lived for 35 years, in the house they'd been letting and near their nephew, Jono and his wife, Bev and family. Several months ago, the letter had arrived when he was alone and he was thrilled to receive it, asking if he'd go and rejoin them in the town, living half a mile from the sea. There was no risk of flooding or erosion from being situated too near the cliff. It was also within walking distance of both the family and what's described as 'all the amenities'. Rory had written back saying he was a bit concerned he was losing his memory. They said they'd do everything to support him. With no parents, they'd love their children to have a grandfather figure, their Uncle Rory. It sounded better with the 'uncle' precursor. They'd so love to have him back near them.

Maggie and he had so enjoyed those years of seeing that part of the family growing up. They were careful not to interfere and step on the toes of Maggie's brother, but some of the best times were truthfully when they went away and Rory and Maggie were asked to keep an eye on their son, Jono and the family. What fun they'd had!

But when their daughter Jen rang to almost beg them move in with her and Mark and their young sons, they realised this was a cry for help they must support. So, he and Maggie had let out their furnished seaside home and taken up residence with this household. Rory had helped to invest in the property, get it electrically sound, plumbing and energy to current standards and even solar panelling. It was extended, decorated and the garden had been rediscovered. He could leave it to them to look further into the electric charger for their next car. It was wonderful together, to give all the family support, but when Maggie failed in health and passed away, Rory was sure he wanted to be somewhere else altogether for his own declining days. He actually yearned to go back home.

"Yes," Rory's attention returned. He asked for a glass of water, while he arranged his thoughts around this important focus. "I want to leave all my part of the house to my daughter, Jen, and family, in the way Maggie and I originally laid down. Then all remaining assets to go to my nephew, Jono and his family."

With what speed the details were clarified, written and signed! The original document would lodge at the solicitor's and Rory had a copy printed off for himself.

Rory finished the glass of water whilst checking his list.

"Is there anything else I can help you with, Mr Adams? Would you like us to send a copy of this new will to your daughter and son-in-law?"

"No, no thank you. I'd prefer to take a printed copy for them, as well as for me. I can give it to them when I'm ready. Please put their name on your business envelope and put c/o me. Then there will be no confusion". No confusion? That was ironic coming from him. "Thank you".

"Here we are, Mr Adams…goodbye and all the very best. It's been a pleasure to know you and Mrs Adams. Here's the name of a solicitor I can recommend, who is near to your seaside home."

"Yes, yes, thank you very much."

Rory stopped off at the client toilets and looked at himself in the mirror. Did he look different? Did the relief that he was starting to feel, show? He opened the solicitor's door, and a waft of air blew in…not quite the sea breeze, but Rory felt it was beginning to blow away all those responsibilities. He was hoping that it would take the worst of the memory loss with it.

Did the sea air still hold miracle cures, acting as a panacea? He did hope so, but even if not for long, he would be reunited with Jono and family and in a special way, to his Maggie. He only needed to take personal items. He would write a letter to his family with instructions concerning anything else they didn't want to go to the charity shops, just as had happened with all Maggie's clothes and remaining personal effects, hopefully to do someone else a good turn…

Rory? He may not be a dog, but he felt a flurry of excitement like, well, a dog with two tails.

* * *

"What's this about?" Rory had waited till Mark and Jen were on their own before he proffered the letter. They scanned it together. Suddenly Rory felt weak. He hadn't considered how upset they might be. After all, he was becoming a bit of a burden, and they very soon wouldn't need him.

"You're moving back to Annest on Sea? But you can't! You're our family here. We can't…we don't want to do without you!"

A flash of chagrin was dismissed as Rory felt his confidence slip away. He remembered his old mother would have declared, "Cat got your tongue?" All these decades later, he could sense her piercing gaze, as he sought the words to explain. Jen tearfully cried "Why didn't you talk to us about this first?" All the bubbling excitement he'd experienced burst. They say that when you have a great boost, something will always come along and burst your bubble.

Of course he apologised. Rory tried to explain that this gave them several months' notice. He'd be here till the end of the long, school summer holidays, to help them out those weeks, when they had to work. It was at this moment that Rory sensed a growing feeling of being unsettled. It was the thought of a new contentedness, of going home that had buoyed him up. Now it was as though a pain of resentment was creeping up from deep within. He told his mind to bury it, as he waited for the shock to abate - theirs and his. How foolish to think it could be straightforward. Rory tried to explain that he thought they might try to dissuade him and then, as though a voice came from outside of him, Rory heard he was speaking out the words, "I feel I want to go back home."

* * *

"Is food ready yet?" The question emitted from three boisterous voices from the hallway, jolted them from their current shock, back to the pragmatic needs of three growing boys. The TV or game they'd been playing had ended. It was unlikely the homework was completed, but they now needed to be fed before the evening's taxi service started for their various activities.

The mealtime was strained, but the banter and noise of the boys carried them all through and, soon enough, Rory was on his own clearing away, with everyone else having left the house. Rory completed the evening's jobs and sat down in his room. Washing over him were bits of the day's conversations and he felt himself drifting off to sleep. He was trying to find someone. He was looking everywhere. And then there she was, smiling. "Come on, they'll get over it! It's our turn to pick up where we left off! It will all be OK."

Rory awoke startled. Where was he? He hadn't seen Maggie so clearly for such a long time. Had he died and found her waiting? Was she speaking of Heaven or Annest on Sea? Any confusion soon vanished with the sound of voices and the general melee of sports kit being dropped amidst the parental shouts of "Don't leave it there, please, put it away!"

"I will later, I'm starving! It's my turn for the last slice of cake!"

"No, now!" But the kitchen cupboards were already banging along with the fridge being raided amidst arguments over who was being greedy and who deserved what. Everyone was back. Rory realised he suddenly felt very tired. He got ready for bed and lost himself in a deep sleep.

* * *

When the boys had finally gone to bed, Jen collapsed on to the sofa. Her feelings rose to the surface and her eyes welled up with tears. Mark brought her over a drink. "It was just such a shock!"

"Yes, but you must have noticed…"

"Noticed what?"

"Your Dad is becoming more forgetful and more frail?"

"No, it's just a bit of old age!" Mark waited before saying fondly, "Rory has done a fantastic job here with us all…but maybe it's time for him to go back. After all, we can still go and visit him! It's not like he'll be a million miles away!" Jen was quiet.

"I miss Mum and I don't want to miss Dad too!" Mark kept his arm round Jen as they sat and finished their drinks.

Jen looked in on her dad. He looked so small in the bed. Then she looked in on their boys who were all sizes, stretched in ungainly angles in and out of their beds. A different thought entered her head…maybe it was time for her dad to have a quieter life, but wouldn't he miss them all and grow lonely? There was a pang of envy considering her cousin and family would have that precious time with her dad, instead of them.

Late June sunlight filtered through the middle of the curtains as Rory awoke to the sound of the morning routine kicking in. He decided to get up and treat it like any other Thursday. Breakfast was the usual chaos with raised voices and thumping of plates and bags and the banging of doors with "Goodbyes" as car doors slammed.

Rory felt he'd done quite well with normality and Jen and Mark had obviously decided to play it the same way, because there was no mention of the evening before.

When everyone had left, Rory rang Bev and she was so delighted, actually crying down the phone. She assured him the tears were of happiness. "What did Jen and Mark say? Were they OK about it?"

"Well, it came as a bit of a shock to them, but they'll get used to the idea. Don't worry. Can you write to those renting the house so I can move back in?"

"Well, you'll never guess the timing! They've written giving us notice that they need to leave in just two months! So, that will give us time to get the place cleaned and decorated. We'll find all the photos you had up, ready for you to come home!" Now it was Rory's turn to have tears in his eyes, picturing Maggie's face greeting him. Yes, he was going home…

Chapter 3
Courage to change

Max was just about managing to manoeuvre the buggy into the allocated space on the No 52 bus, when it got stuck with all the bags sticking out, weighing it down. Freddie started to cry with the pushing and shoving to no avail. The driver said, "Wait a minute, mate," and hopped out of his cab to help free the buggy. Max was so thankful, because he was holding up the queue behind him and Freddie was really having a meltdown. Max delved into the change bag and found a bottle which thankfully soon pacified Freddie. He was due for a feed. We're told that babies are not only aware of their need for food and being made comfortable and comforted, but also arguments and atmospheres. Now Freddie was one year old nothing could escape him. So, Max had decided…

He was so worried about leaving Freddie with Lisa. What with all the drinking and her falling asleep when Freddie was awake. Max wanted Lisa to get help. She insisted there was nothing wrong, but there was. She kept company with the old crowd, who were all the same, just like before. Lisa had promised that everything would change when she had the baby, which did seem to happen while Freddie was still like a toy to her. But then Freddie was more demanding and she started meeting up with the others. Things were spiralling out of control. There was also Jake. Max thought of him as 'Jake the snake'. He'd only met him a couple of times, but he was smooth talking and the way he looked at the girls…They seemed to be flattered by his flirtatious friendliness. Where was all that leading?

Lisa didn't seem interested in Freddie. She said he made her too tired. He needed so much more attention than she seemed willing, or able to give. Max had suggested parents could help her more, especially if she felt lonely. She'd screamed what a terrible mother hers had been, and how his parents just wanted to control them. Max felt so anxious. Perhaps if Lisa was on her own for a bit, she'd see things as they really were. So, Max had been to see a solicitor. He would return to his parents and fight for custody. He didn't know how it would work out, but Lisa now had a record of being drunk and shoplifting booze. She'd originally just had a caution. But then the police had received a complaint from a neighbour concerning raised voices between him and Lisa. In fact, the police had come round when Lisa was collapsed on the floor in a drunken state. While the officers were there, Max had explained the danger; how he was worried what she was doing to herself, but even more so, the danger he feared for Freddie.

The officers looked fed up and annoyed when they'd initially knocked, assuming it was just the 'usual domestic', but recognising Lisa, they could see there was a legitimate problem. Their tone was concerned, and they gave Max the number of a support team.

Well, there was no way now that Max was going to leave anything to chance. He would text Lisa just to let her know that Freddie was OK and he added 'in safe hands'.

* * *

The bus drew to a halt and Max excused himself with the buggy, as he tried to avoid feet and bags protruding into the aisle. He thanked the driver once again who said, "No worries, mate! All the best!" All the best…

Lisa's Mum, Janine, didn't seem one bit like her daughter, but Max had always stuck up for Lisa. His parents, Marg and Pete were different. Even so, he had swallowed his pride when he went round to admit to them that they'd been right all along. He'd been surprised how understanding they'd been. Their faces gave away that they were really relieved. They'd been so worried about Freddie and about Max and Lisa. Then they admitted that several times they'd called round when he was at work and found Lisa unfit to be minding Freddie, but they'd felt powerless to help. He never knew and they were worried about seeming interfering and controlling. Now they'd do anything to support Max's case for custody.

It was with relief and thankfulness that Max arrived at his parents. Freddie fell asleep in his mum's arms. His dad reassured Max that everything would be OK, as they climbed the stairs to what was now to be Max and Freddie's room. It was perfect. They were in the process of sorting out the third bedroom, Max's old room, so when Freddie was settled in his new surroundings they could be in separate rooms. Max reminded them what he was going to do next. His father asked if he'd like him to come with him and wait in the car outside or round the corner. Max thought for a moment and decided it was time to accept all the help he was offered.

Nothing could be more different from where he and Lisa and Freddie had been living. Their flat was on the fourth floor. The stairwells smelt damp and rank, stuffed as they were with leaflets that no one was interested in clearing from the floor and then that whiff of urine, a tell-tale sign left by dogs or cats or whoever. Janine lived in the upmarket end of town. Max felt nervous. Lisa's mother had never been warm towards him, but even less so towards Lisa, who she said was a waste of space. Janine had never given a moment to reach out to Freddie.

Max pressed the doorbell. He waited. Should he press it again? He waited. The house was detached with an orderly garden in front and to the side, where Janine's electric car was on charge. The sweet scent of honeysuckle seemed almost potent in the light drizzle. He felt sick, pulled up his collar and rang again. Footsteps approaching the door sounded like high heels. Max wasn't surprised when Janine opened the door, to see her dressed in a way that could only be described as chic. She inhabited a place a world apart from Lisa, Freddie and him. It wasn't surprising he felt so nervous and inadequate when approaching her.

Janine's face was horrified. "What do you want?" Her eyes darted left to right beyond the door and she yanked him in like a truculent child. Max guessed he mustn't bring down the tone of the neighbourhood, embarrassing Janine with his presence. He took off his trainers, grateful there were no holes obvious in his socks, as Janine glanced down. She stood in the hallway.

"I haven't long, so what is it?" Max had never visited Janine on his own before. They'd never asked for any help, even when Max was between jobs, because Lisa was so adamant about her mother...

Max took a breath. "I wanted you to know I'm very concerned about Freddie's welfare, when alone with Lisa. She won't get help and she's drinking...so I've taken him to my parents. They're very happy to help look after him while I'm at work. Freddie and I are moving there for the time being."

Janine tossed her head. Her hair shone with amber and golden highlights. Pursing her lips she muttered, "So what? If it's money you want, you're not having it for her to waste on drink and drugs!" Max cleared his voice to continue. "No, I'm not here to ask for anything. I just wanted you to know…about Lisa and what's happening. I'm seeking custody. I want Lisa to get help but…"

"Lisa's a waste of space! Always has been!" Janine declared with an expression of disdain, pressing her painted nails across her brow. If my Derek had been alive, he'd have disowned her. It was probably her shocking behaviour that caused his heart attack. I don't want anything to do with her, and I consider this relationship with you as now over." Janine pointedly looked at her watch.

Max felt guilty. He looked Janine in the eye. How had he not managed to help Lisa more? How had it come to this, when perhaps it could have worked out. What could he have done differently? "But would you like me to bring Freddie to visit you?"

Janine's eyes widened as she opened the front door and repeated: "This 'relationship' is now over!"

Max summoned what little confidence he had, as he blurted out, "I wanted you to know, that I've tried!"

Janine said nothing, only opened the door wider and as soon as Max had his trainers on, it slammed with a decisive bang.

Max made his way to his father's car. He was shaking. His father rested his hand on his shoulder as Max wailed, "What else can I do?" He was supposed to be strong, but he felt so tired that he felt like crying, even if 'grown men don't cry'.

His father imagined what response Janine had given Max. "What about Tracey, that old friend of Lisa's?" his father suddenly asked. "I don't know where she lives" Max muttered. "No, but you know where she works? The same salon as Lisa did before Freddie was born?"

An image of the Lisa he'd known smiling, as she blossomed through the pregnancy came to his mind. "Come on, Max, let's try." With that Pete started the car.

Max gazed out of the window. Everyone and everything was going on as usual, but he felt like nothing could ever be the same again. He hoped that somehow, something could turn out better for them all.

* * *

By a stroke of luck, he could see Tracey through the window at the reception desk. "Hiya Max!" Tracey warmly greeted him, but seeing the expression on his face, her brow furrowed and she worriedly asked what was wrong. "Do you have a break? I desperately need to speak to you for a moment?" Max pleaded.

"Hang on!" Tracey slipped to the back and after a moment another member of staff took over and she agreed to come out to sit on a bench that was just up the road. She'd brought them coffees.

Max explained as quickly as he could what had been happening. Tracey's face fell as she listened. The truth was she'd felt so relieved of responsibility when Lisa got together with Max, and she could move out of that horrible flat. It gave her the chance to have a fresh start on her own, with the money she'd inherited. She'd spent many times worrying about Lisa when they were flatmates. She didn't want to go back to that, but, picturing the situation, pushing her own thoughts away, she reassured Max telling him not to worry and promised to go round to Lisa after work.

Max felt relieved that someone else knew – he didn't feel so alone, but leaving Lisa meant that now she was on her own. When they reached his parents, Freddie was playing happily, and Marg seemed in her element. Max felt exhausted. "You go and have a lie down…I'll bring you a cuppa". Max was asleep before the tea was made.

It was Tracey's turn to lock up, so it was 6.00pm before she left, but she'd texted Lisa to say she was popping round. She half expected a text saying the number was no longer available.

Tracey pulled up her collar, shivering with concern. Knocking loudly prompted no reply. Tracey tried again. It was difficult to hear with the noise from neighbouring flats, so she shouted "Lisa!" through the letterbox. There was still no reply, but she could hear the TV playing. After shouting again, she pulled out the door key, which she still had from when they were flatmates. Something had prompted her not to return it.

Tracey felt like she was breaking and entering, even with the key. She gingerly called out, "Lisa!" Tracey felt nervous. What was she going to find? Going from room to room she kept calling, but to her relief there was no awful sight. She didn't find anyone, but just the look of the place, made her feel uneasy. What had happened? She switched off the TV. There was no bag, or mobile anywhere, so Lisa must have taken those with her.

Tracey checked her own phone. No message from Lisa. She texted Max. Perhaps he'd received a text. What should she do now?

* * *

Lisa had always told Max his parents were controlling, and this proved it. That message 'in safe hands'! Huh, right! Max had gone running to them and left her. What right did they have to abduct Freddie - yes, abduct. Lisa reached the local convenience shop and managed to slip a bottle of wine under her jacket. She had every right to cheer herself up. Her friends had shown her the ropes – how to dodge the CCTV cameras. It was a good laugh. It gave her a lift as she wandered home – unaware of the time. What did she care anyway? This was her chance to just do her own thing and…but someone was in the flat. She got out her rape alarm and her scissors - always good to carry some sort of self-defence - and pushed the door open. Right in front of her was Tracey. "What the hell are you doing here?"

Tracey said she had texted her and explained how Max came to the salon and was very concerned about her. She'd let herself in and just found everything as though Lisa had left in a big hurry. "Well, I did." Lisa mouthed with disgust. "They're all out to take Freddie away from me. I'm his mother! I've just seen Max's parents in the park with my baby!" Lisa made no comment about those hollow words which were immediately followed by, "Who cares, wait till they find out what hard work it is to look after Freddie! Then there'll be a different story of happy families!"

"Do you want a cuppa, Lisa?" Tracey asked, moving towards the kettle. "Something stronger!" was the response and out came the bottle of wine from inside her jacket. Tracey's face took on a different look as Lisa laughed: "Fetch the glasses, Tracey. It'll be like old times!"

"No thanks, really, I'd rather have a cuppa as I'm driving!" Tracey quickly replied. Lisa turned away with a flounce declaring, "Suit yourself. I'm going out later, anyway. A tipple now will get me in the mood!" Tracey wondered when Lisa had arranged that time out…what would have happened to Freddie?

Tracey turned her back to make the tea. There was no milk, but she found a teabag and worried about what to say with Lisa in this mood. It was Lisa who spoke next. "Why don't you move back here? It can be the two of us, just like old times?"

"Ah well, you know I've got my own place now," Tracey said feigning brightness, relieved her back was still turned, "and…" Without paying attention, Lisa raved on.

"How about I move in with you then? I could do with sharing a decent place. Where is it again?" Tracey inwardly gulped, imagining that the decent place wouldn't last long once Lisa was there. How unkind to think it, but she knew it was true. "You've got loads of mates round here, Lisa!" Tracey tried to wriggle out of the conversation and move it on. She was desperately trying to think how to change the way it was going, when a raucous clattering broke into the conversation, with people banging on the door. Lisa jumped up and let in a threesome who looked as though they were further down their wine bottle than Lisa, with maybe other things in the mix too. As they picked up their hysterical laughter and turned on the music, Tracey, with one look back, slipped away. Outside was a brightly coloured psychedelic car like something out of the 1960's. You wouldn't miss that easily. She texted Max. "I think you've made the right decision," as she got in her car and drove away.

* * *

Pete and Marg didn't give away the anxiety they felt, anticipating the time ahead. The most important things were to have their son, Max, back and their grandson, Freddie, safe. They were so relieved. They had always felt worried about Max's choice of Lisa. Maybe they wouldn't have stayed together, had she not become pregnant. But they had so wanted her to turn out well as a mother. "It could be the making of her!" was the hope they'd always shared. Of course it was always Lisa's side of the story, but Max gave her the benefit of the doubt, that there hadn't been much love found or lost in the Janine and Derek household. Both Lisa and he were only children without siblings, and there was a connection which led on to their friendship growing and Max had told his parents that he loved her. He believed he could save her from all her old friends and their ways. Tracey had been the only level-headed person they'd met. Marg and Pete could only imagine how grateful Tracey must have felt for Max to rid her of the responsibility of Lisa. That sounded so harsh, but after all the money they had spent on trying to help Lisa, they had to admit, it was pointless. She didn't feel she needed anyone's help. She didn't want anyone's help.

As if knowing he could be safe and settled, Freddie drank and ate and snuggled up whether being held or put in the travel cot. He was so happy. Marg had all kinds of clothes and toys stashed away for whenever they could look after Freddie. Pete was apprehensive about leaving Marg at home alone when he was at work. Lisa's temper could make her unpredictable and if she'd been taking drugs or drinking… What if she turned up on the doorstep?

He and Marg talked about having a camera put on their house and extra locks and they would let the police know. They had great neighbours, who knew how worrying the situation had become and so understood what was happening. They'd be only too willing to take a spare key and to say they'd look out for them. But what about Lisa? After all, she was Freddie's mum. What would Tracey find when she visited Lisa?

After a couple of hours of sleep, Max looked more rested, but drained of colour. He checked his phone for texts and just found one from Tracey saying he'd made the right decision. He sent a message of thanks but with a barrage of queries. What was to become of Lisa? Could he stop feeling responsible? What else could he do? Wasn't it up to the individual to seek help? He'd found already he couldn't make Lisa do that, no matter how hard he'd tried. She was making her own choices.

Marg had cooked a nourishing dinner. His favourite. He couldn't remember the last time he'd just sat down in front of a meal like this, and Freddie was tucking in too. Tomorrow was another day off and Pete suggested they went to the police and explained what was going on, as well as sort out the house's extra security. After the meal, Max listened to the bathtime fun. It just wasn't like this with Lisa. He put his head round the bathroom door and found himself once again near to tears as he thanked his parents. "You go to bed, Max. We'll look after Freddie. By the time he's ready to settle you'll be asleep. Tomorrow's a new day!"

It eased Max's mind more than he'd expected to go to the police and explain what course of action they'd taken. Pete reassured the officer that any one of his colleagues could come round any time to check on Freddie. What the officer didn't say was that Lisa had been picked up the night before with friends, drunk in one of the night clubs, shouting and screaming at security, who were throwing them out.

Pete also took Max back to his solicitor, explaining the urgency of his circumstances. The Administrative Assistant took down some particulars, and said Max would receive a call in the next day or so. Pete also gave his and Marg's number, in case Max was working. Their mood lifted to think this legal process was underway.

* * *

The doorbell rang and Marg anxiously peered through the window of the bedroom where she was changing Freddie. Her heart pounded in case it was Lisa, but to her relief it was Tracey.

She scooped up Freddie and after carrying him down the stairs, secured the stair gate and opened the front door. "Tracey, how lovely to see you, come on in!"

Tracey was visibly upset. "Let's have a coffee!" Marg invited, as she set down Freddie. "You look after Freddie, while I get it."

Tracey had a couple of days off. She'd planned to relax at home and then take a walk in the park on this lovely July day, but she was so tense. Instead, she'd decided to drive past the old flat and just see if there was any sign of life. What she hadn't expected was to find a police car outside. She cried to Marg, "I wondered if I should go in! But I daren't - I care for Lisa, but I don't want to get involved again!"

Marg reassured Tracey that she quite understood, adding that Pete and Max had gone to the police station to explain the situation and to the solicitor. They were unsure what custody would be possible for Max as the unmarried father, but they were going to do all they could to secure it. Certainly, Lisa's mother, Janine, didn't want to be involved.

Tracey explained how she'd found Lisa the evening before, and who knows what was happening this morning?

Freddie climbed round their legs offering them toys and giggled. Tracey found herself relaxing. "Why don't we take Freddie to the park together?" Marg suggested. Tracey looked uncertain. "We could take the No 52 bus to visit Riverside Park at the other end of town, so there'll be no risk of running into Lisa!" Tracey brightened. She was going to have that walk in the park after all, but not on her own. She had a flutter of excitement. It was going to be a real treat.

The driver of the No 52 was cheerful and greeted them with a friendly "Hello" and to their amazement, said: "and it's Freddie, isn't it?" Marg and Tracey looked at each other and back at the driver, who went on, "we've met before on the bus, haven't we Freddie, when you were with Daddy?" That felt like such a lovely surprise.

With a friendly wave back to the driver, Marg and Tracey walked along the river to the park. Tracey realised how lonely she'd been feeling, despite the pleasure of having her own home. Of course, that was only possible because of the inheritance following her mother's death. Coincidentally, just like Lisa and Max, she was an only child, and it looked like Freddie would be too. His chuckle was infectious. She watched Marg's delight in playing with him in the park and thought back to Lisa's vitriolic outbursts concerning Marg's controlling behaviour. Tracey had dropped an envelope through Pete and Marg's door months before and felt so bad to be the bearer of what was assuredly a spiteful letter. Really, it had felt a very long time since she'd been enjoying being with someone around her late mother's age. Don't be ridiculous, she derided herself. You should be moving on in every way. Tracey kidded herself having a partner and the prospect of children wasn't important, yet she was increasingly aware of the biological clock ticking.

"Phew! Lovely to see Freddie's energy! Let's take him back to the buggy for his bottle. I think I need one now!" Marg laughed while she settled Freddie, glancing at Tracey, sensing she was unhappy. "I'm so sorry you lost your mother, and I believe your father died a long time ago?"

"Yes, yes, he did. Triggers go off and I find myself feeling ridiculously sad. I know it's 'normal' but even so, I wish I could move on!"

"You will, you really will, but I've found you don't get over these losses. In time somehow you just adjust to them…"

There was a comfortable silence. Tracey bought them coffee and asked if she could take the buggy, as they strolled back to the bus stop.

"I've really enjoyed this morning despite my emotional outburst!" Marg put an arm round her shoulders and gave Tracey a squeeze. "It's done me the world of good to spend time with you, Marg and Freddie, instead of spending the whole day worrying! I'd love to do this again! Why don't you come and visit me when I'm off next week? But I'm sure you understand, please don't give Lisa my address."

"Absolutely not - and I'd love to bring Freddie!"

It was disappointingly a different bus driver on the way back, but Tracey and Marg chatted on and gave each other a hug before Tracey drove off. She didn't drive straight home, but instead, took herself to a shop she'd often avoided which sold a great range of toys. She immersed herself and then came away excitedly clutching a whole lot of colourful parcels and a lovely box to keep them in. From a really difficult situation was coming some joy, although she realised there would be challenges ahead.

Chapter 4
Route 52: A bus family of regulars

The weather was typical of his mood. Why had he ever thought Renée would want him to stay around? Just because he'd been a shoulder to cry on, didn't mean it would last. He wasn't in her league. She wanted him to change, to find other work. Arthur, being a bus driver, wasn't good enough. Well, this very morning he'd decided. The truth was that it was he himself that would never be good enough. Now Renée had recovered, crisis over, she had her own circle of friends, and he'd never fit in. He didn't really want to try. This job? Well, he felt he was needed. He recognised his regulars, and it was important to get them and all the others travelling where they needed to be. They were like a family to him.

He wondered if other drivers thought about the lives of those who travelled on their buses. No one ever talked about it. Rather, at the end of the shift, they were off. That was understandable having real families of their own, but he would have welcomed a bit of a chat other than about the weather or football. He couldn't help making up stories in his head about his regulars. He fancifully promised he'd write a book one day...as if!

Three of his regular passengers usually sat halfway down the bus. Jean was married to John and then there was her sister, Jenny. For ages the 'three J's' and Jenny's husband Giles had caught together the No 52 into town. It used to be to collect pensions, but now the pensions came directly into their accounts, they just went shopping. Of course, everyone knew the town wasn't what it was. No High Street banks. No shoe or proper clothes shops. At least there was still the post office.

Otherwise, take-aways, cafes, betting and charity shops and boarded-up buildings lined the road. They knew that the more upmarket towns had a better range of 'retail opportunities', still it was their habit to mooch about browsing and then have a coffee and a catch up and, of course, then Giles had died.

On this Wednesday, Jean asked Jenny: "Are you OK? You're very quiet and you do look a bit pale!"

"Well, I don't feel too good today. It's this drizzle I expect!" John thought how it was so 'British' to blame the weather for anything and everything. "Tell us how you're feeling, apart from the weather?" John looked at Jenny, who was like a sister to him too. She did look pale. The bus stopped and as it started up, Jenny slumped. At first he thought it was just the jolt of the bus going forwards, but when she didn't sit up, he grabbed her by the shoulder and with his other arm behind her, eased her back, fearing she'd hurt her head on the handrail in front. "Are you OK?" Jean anxiously asked her sister again, but this time there was no response. "Help, Jenny!"

The person in the seat in front turned round and taking in the scene, jumped up and pushed his way to the driver to ask him to stop. Everyone looked and made way for John and Jean to undo Jenny's top button. "She must have fainted!" John shouted. "Please give her space!"

Jenny had actually had a shock that morning. She'd decided the best thing was to carry on as normal. It had been a terrible year. Firstly, Giles had died. Now her daughter-in-law had announced she and their son were getting a divorce. Jenny hadn't told Jean and John yet. She couldn't bear to put it all into words, because then it would really be true. She just needed to be with her dear Jean and John and now she felt so odd and so weak.

* * *

Strangely enough, Arthur had noticed this lady looked frailer. It was just the way she got on and off the bus. He realised he'd been subconsciously relieved that she'd had her relatives or her friends always with her. The man who used to be alongside her too must have been her husband. He hadn't been around for a while now.

At once Arthur put on his hazard lights and came quickly down the aisle. He felt for a pulse and then called his depot, who would summon an ambulance and a replacement bus. He and the man in front managed to carefully transfer the lady, Jenny, to the aisle floor.

Daphne on the back seat shouted, "Here's some smelling salts!" Whoever imagined in this day and age anyone would carry those around, but Jenny responded a little.

The paramedics carried out neurological tests, having reassured Jean and John that Jenny did at least have a weak pulse. She needed to urgently be taken to hospital. John panicked thinking about the ambulance queues, which the news bulletins showed banking up outside, waiting to deliver their patients into the Accident and Emergency Department. He held Jean's arm, as she held Jenny's hand, until she was whisked away and they caught a taxi to follow the ambulance.

All the passengers had been picked up. Arthur changed the sign to 'out of service' and drove back to the depot, where he filed a report, changed and got into his car. He saw the hospital and instinctively slowed down and drove in. Something made him get a ticket to park up and he walked towards the A&E Department.

* * *

On their arrival, the clinical smell of antiseptic lotions, the murmuring of machines and the bustle of staff had bewildered Jean and John. They lined up at Reception and there explained who they were. They took their seats and waited and waited. What on earth was happening? John went back to the desk. At this point, the receptionist looked at her screen and then caught the nurse. They murmured together and to John's relief, the nurse beckoned to John. He and Jean supported each other, stiff after sitting so long. They followed along the corridor to a cubicle where a screen was pulled round, with voices coming from behind. At which point someone in uniform came out and signalled to John and Jean to accompany him to a room which was clean and vaguely comforting. "I understand that you are Mrs Taylor's sister and brother-in-law?"

"Yes," John and Jean replied simultaneously. "We're Mr and Mrs Seymour."

"I'm so sorry to tell you this, Mr and Mrs Seymour," he spoke gently; "but she's just gone..."

"Gone where?" Jean interrupted frantically.

"I'm so sorry," the doctor continued. "We couldn't save her, she just passed away."

Jean was the elder of the two girls. They'd grown up on the Rogers' family farm, quite as strong as any sons would have been. They'd both loved the country life, as hard as it was and formed a workforce with their parents. It was always the expectation that they'd meet and marry young farmers themselves, but it just didn't happen like that. Instead, Jean's John worked in a builder's yard and Jenny's Giles worked in a garage. They each had one son, and they lived in the same town, where their children grew up together. Jean and Jenny missed the farm and regretted their children didn't have the freedom they'd enjoyed, but then, as it turned out, they'd not seemed the outdoorsy type, in what they knew was called the 'digital age', being happy to meet and play on their Xboxes. Now they both had partners – well Richard, Jenny and Giles's son, was married to Amy, with a delightful daughter, Gillian, the apple of their eye. Jean and John's son Phil was living together with Liz, which it seemed was 'the done thing' now. How they'd missed Giles! That accident was such a terrible shock for Jenny and them all. She'd never quite got over it, well it was still early days…and now? No, there must be a mistake. "Are you sure? Can we see her? It might not be our Jenny behind your screen!"

The doctor led them back and with a nod from the nurse, he took them into the cubicle, where there on the bed was Jenny…their Jenny. Pale but peaceful and so, so still and quiet. It was as though the dam burst, and the year's sadness had suddenly found a way of releasing itself as Jean and John simply couldn't stop their sobs. "I'm so sorry. We believe Mrs Taylor suffered a stroke whilst travelling on the bus this morning, but then another massive stroke here and we just weren't able to save her. Is there someone we can ring for you?" Their minds were a blank, until they both muttered, "Maybe Amy?" Cups of tea came with sugar and biscuits to warm them as they started to shiver. It was just such a terrible shock. They were shown into a relatives' room. "Don't move Jenny yet!" Jean cried and she was reassured that wouldn't happen.

* * *

Arthur gave his name to the receptionist. He looked round at the packed A&E and, while feeling concerned for his passenger, he understood the crisis the hospital and ambulance service were in. It was hot and stuffy sitting amongst all ages of struggling individuals and crying children.

A message was brought to Jean and John that the bus driver had come to see how they were. Would they like to see him. They simultaneously said, "yes please".

Arthur was relieved when the receptionist approached him, saying with a concerned expression: "Mr and Mrs Seymour would be glad for you to join them in the Relatives' Room." So, he was shown in, only to find Mr and Mrs Seymour very upset, having just learnt that their sister, Jenny had died. "Thank you so much for your kindness. We wish she could have been saved, but you acted so quickly. She was just not well."

"Please call me Arthur…I'm so very sorry!" At this point Arthur had to quickly step aside as a young woman rushed past him, like a train derailing. She flung herself on Jean. "Oh, I'm so, so sorry…this is all my fault!" Arthur took this cue to quietly slip away. He found himself standing in the corridor. He suddenly felt very alone. He realised that in an odd sort of way his regulars on Route 52 really had become like family. The passengers would never know. Well, hopefully Mr and Mrs Seymour would know that he cared about them…and about Jenny.

Jean and John looked at each other blankly and back at Amy in alarm. "I loved her so much! She was just like a mother to me," she cried, "and I've let her down. I only told her this morning, how Rich and I, how we're getting a divorce. We're not right for each other now and I'm taking Gillian with me. She'll still see her dad…the courts are working out the custody." The words tumbled out like rocks falling down a waterfall of sobs and tears.

"But what are you going to do? Where are you going to go?"

"Well, you'll never believe what's happened, because it's just unbelievable! I've met someone who's kind and loves us both - and he's a farmer. You really won't believe it…it's such a coincidence, but he bought the Rogers' family farm. I'm going to bring up Gillian there. She'll have the freedom and happiness just like you and Jenny did, and…" With that, Amy burst, inconsolably, into tears.

Jean and John just couldn't take in what they were hearing. It was shock upon shock today. Nothing seemed real.

Jean and John never did their shopping. They were driven home by Amy. No one spoke except in appreciation of the lift. Jean and John sat down at home in their coats. It was as though all their strength had just drained away.

After a while John put on the fire and Jean put on the kettle and then they sat down again. The phone rang. It was Amy. "Are you alright? I've spoken to Rich. He's been in touch with Phil and Liz and they're coming over after work." Jean and John barely registered more than expressing thanks.

The doorbell rang and then the key turned to let in Phil and Liz. It hit Phil how old and frail his parents looked, and a feeling of panic crept up on him, thinking that both his aunt and uncle were now gone and his parents were likely to be next. Grandparents had died long ago.

Richard had confided in Phil, who was more like a brother than a cousin. He stoically stated Amy had found someone else. She had apparently cried that she was sorry, but she wasn't happy. How harsh to be told that when you've married and have started raising a family.

John said it was too late for another cup of tea, but they'd have some toast, so Liz busied herself while Phil asked if they needed to see a doctor because of the shock.

"No, we'll be alright. We just need to have a rest".

"I'll ring you in the morning, Mum." Since Covid, Phil and Liz had moved into a house big enough for them both to have home offices. They had decided they didn't want to marry and they didn't want children. Phil thought of Amy and Rich and shuddered. Maybe he and Liz would drift apart too…these traumas had woken him up to the need to face the present and the future with honesty. It wasn't wise to just drift along. Life was too short. You had to decide to make every day count, while making time for those near and dear to you.

* * *

It was a short walk to the park. There was still time on his parking ticket, so Arthur found himself strolling along the path to the café. He suddenly felt depleted. Buying a late lunch, he ate and 'people watched'. Then, there right ahead of him was a familiar buggy with a lady pushing. Arthur decided that must be a grandparent. But suddenly an angry young woman ran up and started shouting. Arthur felt concerned. It was nothing to do with him – he was only the bus driver, but the accusations and language were disturbing. People were avoiding the scene, and the baby was crying. He realised that he'd heard that same baby's cry recently on a Wednesday morning. He recognised the buggy.

"Can I help?" Arthur asked looking from one woman to the other. "Mind your own business!" the younger one shouted back. But the older looked at him distressed. "Please call my husband. I'm not taking my hands off this buggy!" Arthur took the mobile from her and rang. In no time at all there were footsteps running towards them. The young woman glared, mouthing obscenities and promising to get her baby out of their abducting, controlling hands and then she ran off.

They walked over to the bench, and the older woman took out the baby to soothe him. "Thank you," the older man said. "I only went to the toilets. What made you stop to help? Do you know Freddie?"

"Well, yes and no….is it your son or son-in-law who brings him on the bus? I'm a driver on Route 52. I just happened to recognise the buggy." The man shook Arthur's hand firmly. "That's our son, Max, and this is his son, Freddie. I'm Pete and this is my wife, Marg."

"Thank you so much for going out of your way to help!" Pete said again. "We've a difficult situation to handle. That young woman's Lisa, Freddie's Mum. She won't get help and she needs it - but Freddie and Max are what matters most to us to support and keep safe".

Freddie had a bottle and was asleep. He looked so contented back in his buggy, as the three moved away and Arthur returned to the hospital car park, thinking about the day. Despite the sadnesses and challenges, his mood had lifted. He had made a difference today. He pictured the hospital scene. He wondered what had happened to his other regulars. He thought about the schoolchildren. Many would have finished their exams and wouldn't be back on Route 52. But there would be a whole lot more in the Autumn.

* * *

On his next shift on Route 52 Arthur felt brighter with the morning sunshine, letting go of the sadness of the day before. He was surprised halfway through his route to see Freddie in his buggy getting on the bus with his grandmother and another woman. Well, that's not the mother who was screaming yesterday, he thought, and wondered what had happened. "Why, hello again!" he smiled at Marg. "Oh goodness, what a lovely surprise!" Marg turned to Tracey to explain how kind Arthur had been the day before. "We're going to the far end of Riverside Park today to avoid any run-ins," Marg explained. "A lovely day for a walk in the park!" Arthur smiled, handing them their tickets.

At the next stop a lady climbed on, saying: "I'm new in the area, please can you tell me where to get off for the café end of Riverside Park?" "Yes, you sit up this end, Madam!" the bus driver said.

Brenda was nervous. How ridiculous for someone like her to go on a dating site? She felt embarrassed and a bit ashamed of herself and so sick in her stomach. What had possessed her to get this far?

"Have you just moved into the area?" the driver asked in a friendly manner. "Sorry?" Brenda asked, surprised the driver was making conversation. "I wondered if you were just visiting, or if you'd moved here? It's a lovely locality!"

"Oh yes, it seems to be. Yes, I've not long moved here." Brenda's nerves took over her side of the conversation and she looked out of the window without really seeing anything.

"Here you are, café end of Riverside Park!"

"Thank you!" was all Brenda could muster, as she checked she'd not left anything, but suddenly thought to ask, "Where is the bus stop back?"

"Just over there, can you see the stop by the park sign?" "Oh yes, thank you!". Brenda watched the bus disappear and looked round for the café. She was half an hour early but preferred to get her bearings and arrive on time. It had all been her friend Nancy's idea, but Nancy didn't know she was going through with it. Brenda needed to do this herself, even if right now she felt like backing out of it. Her good manners, though, prevented her from the rudeness of not turning up or sending an apologetic text.

She ambled around the park along the river to the Riverside Café and surreptitiously looked round. No one fitting the man's description was visible to her as she walked on. It was a perfect summer's day and for a few moments Brenda forgot what she was doing and enjoyed the sounds around her. A bench was free for her to do some people-watching whilst also keeping her eye on the time.

In the nearby play area, she could see small children with their grown-ups. One little boy was having a lot of fun under the watchful eye of what looked like a mother and grandmother, who were laughing together. Ah, it must be a mother-in-law and daughter-in-law, she deduced when she heard them each refer to each other with first names. She recognised them as having been on the bus.

Time was up and straightening her skirt, Brenda walked back to the café. Was she wearing the right clothes? Would she pay for her own coffee? Oh no, surely she didn't need the bathroom. Brenda put that firmly out of her mind. "Good morning!" Brenda looked round. "You look like you're Brenda!"

"Yes I am, and you are Nick?"

"Absolutely! Let's have coffee!" Within minutes, Brenda started to relax, but she decided to still be on her guard and not give too much away other than what was in her profile, just in case…

Sunshine greeted Arthur the next day and he was pleased to be on this Route 52, with its pleasant park.

To his surprise, there was the lady again.

"Good morning, how are you?" he asked the lady. "Back to the Riverside Park Cafe?"

"Well yes, please!" Today the lady seemed engaging and more light-hearted. She was obviously feeling more confident in the area. Brenda jumped off the bus and gave him a cheery thank you, before walking on with a spring in her step. The meeting with Nick had gone so well they decided to meet the very next day. Their conversation was friendly and fun. Brenda still was wary, intent on keeping everything under careful control. She'd heard so many bad stories of this kind of relationship and the word 'scams' kept her head reeling at times, from what might go wrong on the internet, over the phone or with all kinds of deals and people, when you weren't being extra vigilant. Nick was equally punctual, and they walked on to have lunch together. Brenda suddenly felt nervous. How stupid to feel lunch was such a big deal over a coffee. But her qualms were soon calmed. Conversation and laughter came easily. Brenda kept searching for any feeling of being 'used and abused' although she felt she was goading herself and overthinking every gesture. Just maybe this friendship was going to work out…a real, new start. She pushed to the back of her mind any niggles she sensed when Nick suggested he picked her up next week and they go out for the day.

Chapter 5
New beginnings

A few weeks had passed, and Arthur was looking forward to lunchtime, when he started annual leave. He wouldn't be going away, but it would be lovely to be free to enjoy this sunny summer.

As passengers climbed on to the No 52 bus, he was surprised to see the newcomer to the area again. She didn't look so bright today. "Good morning, Riverside Park?" he asked. "No, to the shops today". Really, he was ridiculous taking such an interest, but she looked unhappy. She gave him a wan smile as she got off, with a weak wave. He was even more surprised when he went to lunch at his favourite café, when who should he see sitting alone, but the same woman. "We shouldn't keep meeting!" Arthur said. She looked taken aback and he quickly realised she might not recognise him out of uniform, so he showed her his ID and she smiled. "I'm Arthur".

"Oh, I'm Brenda".

"I'm glad to see you smile," Arthur genuinely smiled back. "Forgive me for saying so, but you didn't seem your happy self this morning".

"No, well, I'm just…I've been so stupid…"

"Not moving to this area?"

"Oh no, not that. I've just made a fool of myself!" Before Brenda realised she was pouring her heart out. Arthur was startled and alarm bells started ringing, warning him about his experience with Renée. But he felt so comfortable sitting with Brenda, and she was now looking more like the cheery woman he'd first met on his bus.

They went for a walk from the cafe to the park. It was such a lovely day that they sat on the bench. "Oh look, there's Freddie with his grandmother, Marg!" Arthur declared waving and walking towards them. "Well, how about that, I saw them the other day myself," said Brenda.

"How are you all getting on?" Arthur asked. "This is Brenda. You seem to be having a lot of fun again"

"I saw you the other day with maybe your daughter too?" Brenda joined in the conversation.

"Oh, lovely to see you both, well no, that's not my daughter. She's our special friend, Tracey! She's just parking her car to join us."

The next hour was spent with them all having fun with Freddie, finding themselves so engaged with him and the new friendship they shared. The laughter was broken when an ambulance drove along the road with the shriek of its siren and blue lights flashing. "That's such a shocking sound…you can't help but feel for whoever is in trouble!" they all agreed. That seemed to bring an end to their time, just as the clouds parted and the rain came. "Come on!" Arthur shouted, "I'll give you a lift home!" It didn't even occur to Brenda not to accept the offer, as she had no coat. Before long, they had arrived. What a gentleman, Brenda thought. She suddenly found herself asking if he'd like to pop round one day as he was on leave and, as though it was the most natural thing in the world, the arrangement was made.

Tracey gave Marg and Freddie a lift too. Tracey hadn't told anyone how far she'd gone with buying things for Freddie, including a car seat. Marg was amazed she had one, but Tracey just laughed it off without an explanation. Turning a corner, the traffic had stopped. How strange. Freddie was asleep, so there was no worry, but Marg could see through her passenger window that the ambulance was ahead. "Oh no, what's happened on the bridge? Some vehicle has gone too close and collided again! That must have been the ambulance we heard..." After a while a police officer approached all the waiting cars and explained there had been an accident.

"I'm afraid you'll be here for a while to come".

"What's happened?"

"I'm very sad to say that there's been a collision". The officer walked on to speak to the other drivers.

"How far can you see?" Tracey questioned urgently.

"Only as far ahead as the cars involved and the emergency vehicles," Marg said.

Freddie was stirring and Tracey was concerned how long they may be there. She got out of the car to see for herself, and it felt like her heart stopped when she saw the mangled psychedelic car ahead. "Oh no! No, no!" Tracey shrieked, but slammed her hand over her mouth so not to let out another scream. Tracey climbed back in and slumped in her seat. "What's wrong? What's happened?" Marg repeated.

"One of those cars in the collision....it belonged to Lisa's friends".

Freddie awoke and started to cry. They decided that Marg would get out of the car and walk on with Freddie in the buggy, as there was no knowing how long they'd be in the queue. She'd maybe find out something more and text Tracey. Marg was told to go back, as the bridge was completely impassable, so she explained to Tracey as she passed by that they would catch a bus, and they promised to keep in touch. It was too soon for anything on the local news. When Marg spoke to Pete and Max later, they decided to go to the hospital to find out what they could, explaining who they were, while Marg looked after Freddie. Had Lisa been in that car?

* * *

After the afternoon's rain, it was a beautiful summer evening. Nevertheless, Max felt himself shiver as they parked up at the hospital and approached the A&E reception desk. Pete put his hand on Max's arm and stepped forward to explain why they were there. They were asked to sit down while enquiries were made. After just a few moments, a member of staff in scrubs approached them, checked their names and asked them to go with him. They followed down corridors until they reached a room outside the Intensive Therapy Department.

"I am Greg, one of the Critical Care nurses. Let me be sure I understand exactly that you, Mr Max James, are the partner of Lisa Bennett? And you are Max's father?" "Yes, yes, that's right," Pete replied for both of them.

"We're glad you have come in. As you know, there was a collision on the bridge this afternoon. There were four individuals in one of the cars. Very sadly two travelling in the front were killed, as was the driver in the other vehicle. Two travelling in the back are critically ill, here in Intensive Care. One we know as Lisa Bennett, although she had no documents on her which gave other contact details."

Max's voice caught as he asked, "How is Lisa?" Greg took his time to answer. "I am sorry to say she was very badly injured, and the next few hours will be critical". Pete and Max's faces blanched. "What can we do? Can we see Lisa?"

"Yes, but just for a few moments. It will be a shock for you – are you sure you're OK to do this?" Max and Pete insisted they must, and waited while Greg let them into the IT ward. The clinical smells and bleeping of machines struck them. Voices seemed subdued, although there was plenty of activity surrounding each of the beds. Greg led them over to the bedside, where Lisa could barely be seen for tubes and intravenous infusions. "What's happened to her?" Max asked, his eyes filling with tears. "Lisa has broken a number of bones, but it's the internal injuries that are of most concern".

"But how?"

"I'm afraid it seems that all may have been under the influence of alcohol and drugs. Would that have been unusual?" Max felt himself falling and was quickly helped to the bedside chair and brought a glass of water. Pete found himself stuttering, "No, no it wouldn't be unusual".

Greg said he would be back in a few moments. When he returned, he led them to a visitors' room, where he took down some contact details and other particulars and promised they would be telephoned. They were recommended to have a cup of tea before leaving the hospital.

Pete messaged Marg to say they'd be home shortly and would explain what had happened then. Freddie was already asleep. Marg took one look at their faces and put her hand over her mouth before muttering, "No, was it Lisa? What's happened?" They explained all they knew. The three of them sat in silence, before Max rang Tracey to let her know the news. She said she would come straight round.

The four of them sat drinking tea, as they watched the clock. Just as Tracey was thinking about going home, Max's mobile rang. "It's the hospital. They advise us to come in."

Pete drove both Max and Tracey and the three went straight to the IT ward.

They were all let in, although the rule was usually two visitors at a time. Max found himself holding Tracey's hand, as they approached Lisa's bedside. A nurse giving her name as Amanda explained Greg had gone off duty, so she was looking after Lisa. She went on to say that Lisa's observations were showing she was struggling. With that, the buzzers went off and they were ushered from the ward to the room where they'd met with Greg earlier.

The three stared at the walls with its restful décor and framed calming pictures, which didn't reflect their mood one bit. The door opened and Amanda entered with a mask round her neck and sad eyes meeting theirs. "I'm so very sorry. We couldn't save Lisa..."

* * *

In just a few hours, the world had changed again. Tracey found herself shaking. Max naturally put his arm round her. They sat like that until Amanda returned, asking if they'd like to see Lisa.

They stood up. The screens were round Lisa's bed. They hesitated, but then Max went forwards. All the tubes had been removed and the intravenous bottles taken away. Lisa was simply lying in the bed peacefully, as though she was asleep. Amanda brought two more chairs, and they all just sat and looked at Lisa, lost in their own thoughts.

Amanda explained what would happen next, before they left. Max kept thinking of his last conversation with Lisa…and with Janine. How he'd messaged Lisa to say Freddie was in safe hands. The same wasn't true for Lisa. He shuddered to think that Freddie could have been in that car too. Odd thoughts went through his mind. When the solicitor rang, there would be another change of circumstances for the paperwork.

Marg invited Tracey to stay the night, so she wasn't on her own. Pete could drive her over to pick up her things. Tracey felt like this wasn't real. It must be the shock of everything, but a strange feeling had come over her. She wanted…she needed to be with this family. She had shared history with them. She felt she belonged

PART 2
December

Chapter 1
Going back, to go forwards

"You must go back and see your mum!" Lin looked at Gemma's distraught face. "I've messaged her to say I'm fine and told her where I am!" Gemma exclaimed. "I can't bear to go back!" It had been six months, and Gemma's mother had left her messages during the last few weeks which had upset her. Luke had tried to reason with her, but she kept making excuses not to talk about it. He asked his mum to try. Lin and Chris had talked it over, so Lin added, "We'll all come with you in the Christmas holidays. I know what you told us and maybe there's a lot more besides, but now maybe your mum just needs to see you."

This touched a nerve. Gemma had started to worry the same thing, but she was so afraid of going back and getting trapped into staying. She dreaded seeing Jez again. Her job had worked out. She and Luke were so happy. It was such a relief to live safely and freely and to breathe the sea air. But the offer of support from Luke and his parents coming with her encouraged Gemma at last to reconsider. "OK, if you really will come with me and not leave me there! You can't realise how it feels to be away. I just can't face being forced back!" Lin put her arms round Gemma and promised they would bring her back home to the Isle of Man. While her face was turned away, Gemma couldn't see the concern that Lin showed. The last months had been so stressful, with the major fraud case she had become entangled with, but there was nothing to prevent them leaving the Island for a few days now. In fact, Lin was glad for a good reason to do so.

Since that last journey on the No 52 bus, Gemma's new life had preoccupied her. It was very special to be part of Lin and

Chris and Luke's family. In fact, she realised that since her dad had died, she'd just never felt she belonged. It was alarmingly quickly that Gemma's mum, Tricia, had partnered with Jeremy, Jez. At first, she was relieved that her mum had seemed happier again. But that changed when Jez moved in. To start with she'd thought she was imagining his attention and his flattering comments, but that turned to him criticising her, what she wore and wanting to always know where she was going and who she was with. Gemma felt so uncomfortable. In time that turned to anxiety, concerning if ever she should find herself on her own in the house with him.

It couldn't have worked out better when she and her mum were looking through breaks away at a good discount and her mum was excited about an offer, which would mean she and Jez could have a holiday. Gemma realised that when they left, it would be the day after she'd finished her exams, so everything would come together to help her to get away herself. She just hoped it would happen as planned.

* * *

Arrangements were made by Chris for their flights back to the 'adjacent island', as the Manx called England, and a stay in a hotel. Luke was concerned how pale Gemma looked and hardly a word was spoken on the journey. He held her hand firmly as they walked through to collect their hired car. After the simplicity of the small Ronaldsway airport, Gemma felt overwhelmed. She couldn't believe she'd made the outward journey on her own with such expectation and now she returned with such dread. The crowds of people, the volume of noise and the flashing of numerous lights made her feel nauseated. It was only 4.00pm but approaching the shortest day, it felt like midnight, it was so dark. The plan was to visit her mum to take Christmas presents in the morning.

Hail and sleet hammered down against the windows all night. Gemma tossed and turned, checking the clock almost on the hour every hour. Luke slept soundly and she cast him regular glances. Did he really love her? Her chest tightened. The nightmare in her head told her this trip was a set-up to dump her back where she supposedly belonged. At that moment, she didn't know why, something of the confidence and calm she'd previously carried within her returned. Well, if that fear was realised, she would find another way to start over somewhere else. She now had a bit more money saved, so she could begin again. She was determined never to go back.

The alarm clock still startled her, but Gemma jumped into the shower. She woke Luke and went down for breakfast, feeling more like herself. Lin and Chris were relieved to see her looking brighter, and they sat by a window as the skies cleared and a wintry sun dared to show its face. When Luke joined them, the travel plan had been checked, and Gemma messaged her mum with their estimated time of arrival for lunch.

* * *

Gemma pushed aside any anxiety about the shabbiness of her mum's home, in contrast to Lin and Chris's extravagant house and indeed the flat which she and Luke had made together. It had been such fun finding pieces of furniture and Lin had helped with the soft furnishings. Gemma loved scouring the charity shops for bargains and in no time, the flat was colourfully and tastefully made into their first home.

Tricia opened the door and threw her arms round Gemma, almost knocking her off her feet. In contrast, there was a polite handshake and thank you to Lin and Chris accepting the flowers they had brought and just a hand on Luke's arm, steering him through to the sitting room. There was no Jez. While Tricia finished laying out the buffet with Lin's help, Gemma excused herself and went upstairs. Firstly, she glanced in her room which was exactly as she'd left it. Then the bathroom, and then she peered into her mother's bedroom. It didn't look like it had before. It strangely seemed as though it was only occupied by her mum.

Over lunch, there was superficial conversation. Then Tricia sat down and, with an anxious glance around the three faces turned to hers, she declared there needed to be an explanation.

"There's no point beating about the bush!" Tricia took a breath and spluttered. "Please let me just get out what's happened. Don't ask me any questions yet, or I'll never get through this!" Gemma felt her stomach lurch and gripped Luke's hand all the more strongly. She couldn't look at Lin and Chris. This was all way beyond her control.

"Gemma, I'm so sorry to have brought Jez into your life. I know it was because of him you ran away, well, you wanted to leave, but you wouldn't have gone like that if…" Her voice trailed off. "I was so afraid he would hurt you, that I thought if we went on that holiday, somehow it would change him for the better." Gemma was incredulous. Her mum had actually realised the anxiety she'd been living with, but had never said anything.

"If I'd said anything to Jez, well, I don't know what would have happened. He was OK to start with, quite excited to be away, but then he started wandering off in the evenings and leaving me or going out in the daytimes on some pretext or other. Then I followed him." Gemma couldn't believe her ears. It sounded like her mum was in some sort of police drama. Help! History was repeating itself. "It was just as I'd thought, even after he moved in with us. He was meeting up with some girl or other. I didn't know what to do. I didn't know where to turn to for help. I felt so stupid and ashamed. I just wanted rid of him! You could say that as luck would have it, on the last night Jez got really drunk and involved in a brawl. He'd hit the girl he was with, and the police were called by a bystander. He was arrested. I felt sick when the police interviewed me at the hotel, but secretly I was pleased. I was relieved. I told them what he was like. They found on his phone horrible images. I can't bear to think of it. I was terrified Jez would blame me for getting him in trouble. I told them I was afraid for you, that even though you'd run away, you might come back, or he might try to find you himself."

Gemma felt her eyes sting. How terrible her mum's life had become. "Anyway, Jez was in far more trouble than one brawl. I can't dare to think of the terrors he's caused. I was just a base for him, a naïve woman who was lonely and fell for his charm, but not so completely on my own as it turned out. There was a real 'domino effect' once they started questioning him. He's in prison now, for a good long time, I hope. When I messaged you, I didn't know what was happening, but he's gone now. I so wanted to see you and to explain, because I'm moving out. I'm going to Auntie Liz's until I can find somewhere of my own. I'm not so scared now for you or for me or for anyone. I desperately want to know you're OK and I need you to realise how sorry I am to have put you through that nightmare of a man. I need you to look through your things. I'll send them on to you. I don't even know how your 'A' level results turned out. I was so worried they'd go wrong because of everything happening here."

It seemed surreal to be talking about how well she had done in her school exams which seemed a lifetime ago. As she described how happy she was, Tricia burst into tears, as all pent-up feelings poured out. Gemma jumped up to put her arms round her mum, while Lin made another cup of tea. Why is it everyone drinks tea in a crisis? Once she'd caught her breath, Tricia brought out some Christmas presents. "I have something for you Gemma, in fact for you all. They're hopefully not too big for your cases." Lin and Chris unwrapped a most beautiful small wooden box in the style of a cupboard. On the door the words carved read 'the treasure is within'. Inside was an exquisite miniature vase. What extra meaning was hidden in that gift? For Luke, Tricia had framed a lovely photo of Gemma, the last one taken when she looked happy before her dad died. For Gemma, there was a photo album of her and her parents and the framed painting she'd always loved of a sea view.

Gemma gave her mum a framed photo of her and Luke, and they chatted much more freely now that so much had been shared. Gemma went upstairs to sort out the things in her room which she wanted her mum to send on to her, leaving Tricia talking together with Luke, Lin and Chris. A few minutes later, Gemma felt an arm on her shoulder, and she suddenly jumped. The fear rose in her until she realised that it was Luke and not Jez. He wrapped her in his arms and sat her down on the bed. "I'm so sorry to hear about everything. You and your mum have been so brave and now you can both start again with a happy life."

"Yes, but are you sure you want me, Luke, because I so want my life to be with you?"

"I think I can reassure you of that!" Luke took out a small box and opened it. "I've just actually asked your mum, Gemma, and she's very happy. Will you marry me?" Now it was Gemma's turn to burst into tears. "What about your mum and dad? Will they be OK about us?"

"Don't worry about them, they've loved you from the start!"

Gemma and Luke went downstairs. Smiles met them. They were all in on the excitement. The engagement ring sparkled and fitted perfectly.

As they prepared to leave, Gemma promised to keep in touch. As she turned over the painting her mum had given to her, she exclaimed, "Oh, I don't believe it! I never knew there was a place name scratched on the back. It's of the coast in Castletown on the Isle of Man!"

"I never realised that either!" laughed Tricia. "I guess you're taking it home…"

Chapter 2
Home sweet home

The sea breeze blew the sand into his face, as Rory strolled along the beach walking his dog, Jeffrey. How he loved this, whatever the weather. Rory had laughed as they'd chatted over the fence during the early autumn. He'd told his young neighbours how people joked his name sounded like a dog's. Jeffrey had always seemed so delighted to see him, that he offered to walk him in the mornings when they had gone to work. Then one morning they'd dropped the bombshell. They had the opportunity to work abroad and didn't know what to do about Jeffrey. Rory had grown very fond of their dog, so when they asked if he would consider Jeffrey becoming his own, he was delighted. He did explain that he was already 84, but Jeffrey was ten himself as he'd been a rescue dog, not theirs from a puppy. That made him feel easier about the lifespans they shared. Rory was about to 'rescue' him again.

At first when Jen and Mark visited, there had been an awkward atmosphere. They were missing him living with them. But Jeffrey seemed to break the ice and their boys loved him too. Rory felt his memory improving, as he was less stressed. In fact, he felt he had a new lease of life. Maybe it was partly the sea air! His Maggie would have been so surprised. They'd never had a pet, and he really couldn't remember now, why not.

Rory returned home and to his astonishment there was a cat in the garden. Jeffrey barked but wagged his tail excitedly. It was in the evening when Jeffrey was having his last visit to the garden, that Rory heard him barking again. He could just make out Jeffrey in the half-light, so went outside only to find him wagging his tail near the cat, who was now miaowing. "What are you still doing here?" Rory asked approaching the cat, who immediately stood and curled itself round his legs. It didn't seem worried about Jeffrey at all. "I didn't think cats and dogs were supposed to get on!" Rory smiled. "Where do you belong?" Rory stroked it and walked back inside, leaving the door ajar for Jeffrey. He closed the door only to find the cat had slipped into the kitchen with them. "Hey, what are you doing here?" Rory couldn't help bending down to stroke the cat which purred and wound itself round his legs again. Jeffrey wagged his tail and gave out some little yelps. "Are you trying to talk?" Rory wondered what to do. He must find the cat's owners, but it was dark now. It would have to wait till the morning. Meantime what could he feed it?

Rory looked in his cupboard and found a tin of tuna and decided that would have to do and a saucer of milk. He sat close to Jeffrey, in case he showed too much interest in the cat feeding, but it was extraordinary how he seemed to know that this was the cat's supper! Without hesitation, it ate and drank and then washed itself. Jeffrey in the meantime had settled down with his head on his paws watching. Rory picked up the cat's dishes and found a blanket which he put down on the kitchen floor near to Jeffrey's bed. He'd leave them with some water and just see what happened. Rory didn't hear a bark or a miaow. He got up to the bathroom and couldn't resist peeping through the glass kitchen door. To his amazement, Jeffrey was on the blanket, and the cat was in his bed!

In the morning, Rory let out the cat with Jeffrey, thinking the cat would take off having had a sleepover with them. He was so surprised that both came back in looking for breakfast, so Rory repeated the previous evening's meal. The cat was very pretty. It was tabby, not unlike Jeffrey in colouring, with lovely white markings round its brown eyes. There was no collar, and he wasn't sure about microchipping. Could you see a microchip?

After his own breakfast it was time to walk Jeffrey. He had an idea. He would take a photo on his phone, let out the cat and knock on all the neighbours' doors down the road to ask if they knew the cat. Maggie would be so proud of him using a mobile phone. In fact, he never had till he moved back, but Jono made the time to show him how it worked, and he loved it for messages and even playing one or two games. There was nothing wrong with his eyes!

No one recognised the cat. Rory found himself expecting the cat to have gone, although secretly hoping it hadn't. But there it was, and it happily ran to meet Jeffrey and him, purring round Rory's legs. So, Rory sent a message to Jono asking him to pop round assuring him there was nothing wrong. Jono was incredulous – first a dog and now a cat, but Rory assured him he wasn't going to keep it, although he laughed describing how well Jeffrey had taken to the cat and the previous night's sleeping arrangements. The cat was so sleek and didn't look like a stray. Someone must be so worried to have lost it. Jono put a photo and message on the local Facebook page, asking for anyone to make contact if they'd lost the cat.

* * *

The next day was Saturday. Rory took Jeffrey for his walk and when he came back, a couple got out of their car and approached him. They seemed upset. "Oh, you have Millie!" the woman exclaimed.

"Millie? Is that your name?" Rory turned to the cat, who was now sitting on the doorstep. "Why don't you come in?" Rory invited. "Let's have a cuppa!"

Once seated in the kitchen with cups of coffee, Jack and Megan explained they'd been worried sick. They had been cat sitting for Jack's brother and wife, who had left at short notice, as her elderly parent had suffered a serious fall. There had been a frantic telephone call leading to rushed arrangements. The most crucial point was not to let the cat out, as it was not allowed to leave the house. Megan was signing for a parcel delivery and that's when Millie must have slipped out. Jack and Megan didn't know the area, but they'd searched everywhere and finally visited the vet's, who were going to place an SOS on the local news. Then they'd found the message on the local Facebook page, which Jono had posted.

As they paused in conversation, all eyes turned to Millie, who was back in Jeffrey's bed, where his chin was resting against her. "Oh!" they simultaneously let out a cry of relief with surprise. "Well of course, they used to have a dog," Jack declared, but they had to let it go last year. It was a different breed from yours, but about the same size."

A silence full of unspoken words filled the air. Jack and Megan then fetched the cat basket from the car and proceeded to lift Millie into it. Even their gentle murmurings didn't stop her from trying to fight her way from their hands. Not helping, Jeffrey barked and jumped up and down in front of the basket and at the door, while they drove Millie away. He only stopped when Rory shut the door and sat back down at the table.

Often Rory went round to Jono and family on a Saturday afternoon, but somehow, he just didn't feel like it. How can you say that a dog looks sad? Well, Jeffrey did. Is that what 'hangdog' means, Rory wondered? Jeffrey didn't even eat his supper. In fact, to Rory's amazement, he didn't go back in his bed. Instead, he lay down on the blanket resting his chin on the side of it. The whole home seemed to have lost its sparkle. Rory rang Jono to thank him for the success of his message on the local Facebook page, saying he was fine, but he had some things to do that afternoon. Really, he just wanted time on his own.

* * *

The next morning Rory went to church, which was a very important part of his week and there to his surprise were Jack and Megan. "Good morning! How are you?" Rory asked, settling down on the pew next to them before the start of the service. "Actually, we've had barely a minute's sleep!"

"Oh no, what's wrong with Millie?" Rory anxiously asked.

"We think Millie's missing you and Jeffrey!" Rory's heart missed a beat, as he felt the same about Millie. Extraordinary though it seemed, in such a short time, he'd grown to love the cat, partly because Jeffrey had taken to her so well. "How long are you here for?" asked Rory.

"Well, that's the problem. The news isn't good". There wasn't going to be a quick fix. Jack's brother and wife needed to stay on for the time being and with so much going on with her parent, they didn't know what to do with the cat. "We can't stay indefinitely, either, because we usually look after our grandchildren every week!"

Without hesitation, Rory said, "I'd love to help look after Millie, but she's already used to going outside. Tell your brother and see what they think". They exchanged telephone numbers and as the service started, while Rory prayed for the elderly relative, he also laid out the earnest wish he had for Millie to come to live with him and Jeffrey.

Rory couldn't settle. He and Jeffrey went out for a walk on a Sunday afternoon. This was something that usually gave him great pleasure. Today the early sun had disappeared, and chilly drizzle seemed to reflect his and Jeffrey's mood. On reaching home, it was a rub down for Jeffrey, before Rory noticed a message on his answerphone. He couldn't help a flutter of excitement, but what would the news be?

To his delight, Jack's brother was only too pleased for Rory to be Millie's adoptive parent, along with Jeffrey. They were apparently happy for her to be let outside if she was finding her bearings. He and his wife had taken the decision to rent out their home and stay on indefinitely to care for the elderly parent. Rory immediately did a call back.

"Well, my nephew and I know all about letting a house in this area. My late wife, Maggie and I did it ourselves." Rory told them the agent's details they'd used and then he asked when Jack and Megan would like to bring round Millie.

"Right away, if that suits you! She won't stop miaowing and glaring at us!" Rory laughed and excitedly cleared space in his utility room for cat food and any other items Millie would bring with her.

The doorbell rang and clawing to get out of the basket was Millie. As soon as it was open, she jumped out and ran into the kitchen, followed by Jeffrey. Rory took a photo of what could only be described as a loving reunion, which he said he'd send to Jack and Megan so they could forward it to Millie's owners and Jono could put it on the local face book news. Later, after his pets had finished their supper and been outside for a visit, Rory peeped in the kitchen. This needed another photograph. Rory could hardly stop his hand shaking as he chortled, capturing the two curled up in Jeffrey's bed together. Now

Rory truly felt like a dog with two tails, or maybe the cat who's got the cream!

* * *

A few weeks later it was Rory's 85th birthday. He'd invited Jono, Bev and family and Jen and Mark and the boys were coming over. Rory so hoped that any awkwardness would disappear between the two families, following his move back to Annest by Sea.

There was such delight when they all greeted Jeffrey and Millie, and the conversation was flowing freely between the children. They all enjoyed tea with the traditional birthday cake and only a few candles to make the birthday wish, which Rory already felt had come true. Rory had plenty of puff to blow them out, due to his daily walks with Jeffrey.

It was when Jen came into the kitchen to have a quiet word that Rory took a deep breath, but he needn't have worried. She was smiling. "You know Dad, Jeffrey and Millie have given you a new lease of life! You look so well and happy! Moving back here was obviously the right thing for you to do and I'm sorry I was miserable and mean about it. I was being selfish and really the boys have grown up a lot having to be more independent. You'd not believe how they help out - well, when they're in the mood!" Rory smiled at the memories and was pleased that the timing had turned out just right.

"Look at your magnetic noticeboard on the fridge! Today it's only got cat and dog food listed!" Jen laughed.

"Oh, that's to remind them I haven't forgotten them. They do understand everything, you know!" Rory justified himself. "I don't use lists like I used to, but it's a handy reminder every day to check the board."

Jen remembered how Mark had said her dad was losing his memory. Well, it seemed the sea air had blown all the cobwebs away. His mind was so clear. "It only takes us two and a half hours to get here, so there's no need for me to fuss about it and the boys are all enjoying getting to know Jono and Bev's family. You've opened up so much for us and, I don't know, just looking round at the photos of you and Mum. It is so lovely to see her smile here again. We want to take a photo of us all!" So, they all posed, and several were taken to try and capture everyone looking in the right direction and some without ridiculous faces! They also took a couple of Jeffrey and Millie. Once they'd left, Rory sighed, but not with any regret, rather, a real contentment. What had Maggie said to him? "Come on, they'll get over it! It's our turn to pick up where we left off! It will all be OK."

When the framed photograph arrived several days later, Rory found to his delight that there was also one of Jeffrey and Millie happily together. Rory hung them on the wall between Maggie and himself and one which said, 'Home sweet home'. Yes, he'd come home.

Chapter 3
New life, new happiness

Max was shaken by a whole range of different emotions. Shock, sadness and grief at the loss of Freddie's mum, Lisa. It was complicated by the feelings of relief he tried to bury. The months of anxiety concerning Lisa and Freddie's welfare now seemed to have been replaced by a nagging remorse and worry that he'd let Lisa down.

When he'd gone to tell Lisa's mum, Janine, about the accident and to ask if she would like to be involved in planning the funeral arrangements, he'd been met by a seemingly emotionless, stony face. "I take it that's a 'no' then," he'd spluttered through his own tears. Janine had shut the door in his face. That was that then. Max was so very thankful that he had the support of his own parents and their genuine love for for him and Freddie.

The bedrooms were now organised so he and Freddie had one each. A few pieces of furniture had been merged in his parents' home, but most of the furniture from his and Lisa's flat had gone to charity from where most had originated. Tracey had been a wonderful help going through Lisa's clothes and personal possessions and disposing of them. It was painful looking at old photos, so Max asked Tracey to sift through them. She had made albums for Max and Freddie of the best of them, so they could share the good memories, as Freddie grew up.

It was while Tracey did all this, in her spare time from the salon, that she found she was spending much of it with Max. Sometimes they were able to smile, but the rest of the time there was a sadness in Max's eyes. Tracey realised that any happiness made Max feel guilty. When Tracey looked back at photographs of them as friends, she realised that she had feelings for Max which had grown. She told herself firmly that this was all due to the shock and shared loss. Tracey was also keeping company with Pete and Marg, who even planned any appointment. for when she could look after Freddie. How much she looked forward to those special times and now a spare room was set aside for toys and spare clothes for Freddie.

Tracey became fearful of what she realised was a growing love for the whole family. She was scared and decided she must rein in her feelings and get everything in perspective before she was really hurt. After all, there was no future in what she found herself imagining. The feelings could never be mutual. Yet, Tracey found herself hoping and even praying that something would happen to change the present and indeed the future.

Max seemed to have spent the last few months in a daze. He was back at work fulltime and was always thanking his parents and Tracey for all they were doing to help him and Freddie, explaining he couldn't have done without them. Freddie was flourishing. But Max couldn't get rid of the sense of guilt he had, of not being able to save Lisa from that fatal crash. Leading up to her funeral, the vicar had visited to make the arrangements. He was about the same age as him and easy to talk to. He'd given Max his mobile number and suggested he could call him to meet up, if he'd like to do so. One day, Max found the card in his wallet and rang the number, expecting it to go to voicemail. To his surprise the vicar answered and Max explained who he was. The vicar remembered exactly, and they arranged to meet for a coffee the following Friday after Max's work.

* * *

Over the following days, Max several times almost cancelled the meet-up, but he couldn't think what to say. In fact, that was the main reason for cancelling anyway, what was he going to say? The day came and nervously Max arrived at the coffee shop, where the vicar was already sitting tucked away in a corner, reading a book. The vicar shook Max's hand warmly and invited Max to call him Ed. After exchanging pleasantries, once their coffees had arrived, Ed sat and waited a few moments, before asking how Max really was doing. It seemed easy to speak to Ed. Max realised that he could put into words what he was feeling – that he couldn't forgive himself for failing Lisa and Freddie and feeling guilty at his sense of relief, that the struggle was over.

Ed seemed to understand perfectly. He returned to some words he'd read at Lisa's funeral. He quoted from the Apostle Paul's letter to the Romans chapter 8, verse 1:

"There is no condemnation for those who are in Christ Jesus, because through Christ Jesus, the law of the Spirit of life set me free from the law of sin and death."

Max listened again to Ed reciting the words and explaining that Jesus Christ had taken the punishment for all our mistakes and shortcomings by dying on the cross. Jesus had overcome the power of all darkness and pain by rising from the dead. Max found himself asking, "but what about Lisa?". She was now dead.

Ed then opened a bible he had with him, finding a passage later in the very same chapter of the book of Romans, verse 38: "For I am convinced that neither death nor life, neither angels nor demons, neither the present nor the future, nor any powers, neither height nor depth, nor anything else in all creation, will be able to separate us from the love of God that is in Christ Jesus our Lord."

And then, something happened. From deep within a sob came up and Max found himself crying. He had no embarrassment. He didn't worry if anyone could see him. A tremendous sense of reassurance spread through him.

"I needed to know this," he spluttered. Ed sat with Max saying nothing. He knew that Max was processing something profound. After a while, Max looked up from having his head in his hands and asked if Ed would pray with him.

"I want to keep hold of this feeling of release and thankfulness to Jesus for all he's done for me and all of us and Lisa. For the first time I'm starting to understand about something I've never thought of before. Is this faith?"

"Yes, Max, this is faith…believing in forgiveness, a new start and the love God has for you and everyone, which never leaves."

"I want this for me and for Freddie and for…" Ed prayed that Max would know the reality of a relationship with the Lord Jesus in his life. "What do I do next?"

"Come to church with Freddie on Sunday!"

* * *

Max felt lighter and happier than he could remember as he walked home. Marg and Pete had been anxiously waiting to know the outcome of his meet-up. They were astonished to hear what had happened. "Mum, Dad, will you come with Freddie and me to church next Sunday?" They looked at each other and were lost for words. But then Pete said, "Of course we will, son, anything to help you and Freddie".

Later that night Marg and Pete talked quietly about how they felt a bit uncomfortable about going to church. They'd only been to weddings and christenings since their own wedding. They both realised they'd felt a bit guilty about that, but weren't sure why and anyway, they'd always been busy on Sundays.

The next day, Max decided to meet Tracey when she finished at the salon. She was so pleased, as he'd never done that before. She was very surprised when he invited her to come to church. "Ed says it doesn't matter that we've not been before. Mum and Dad are coming too. We can put Freddie to play in the crèche if he's restless." Tracey was feeling two distinct convictions. One was that she could always go in the crèche with Freddie. The other was recalling how she had found herself hoping and even praying that something would happen to change the present and indeed the future.

The service didn't start till 10.00am so there was no stress in them all getting to the church. Tracey met them there, so they could go in together. Someone on the door welcomed them in and showed them where the crèche was if they wanted Freddie to go and play there, explaining all the helpers had DBS checks and would always fetch a parent if a child was unhappy. There was a relaxed feel, and they were shown where they could sit together. Max didn't know what to expect, but he was amazed to see music stands and microphones, with instruments, including a drum kit. There was a screen, and notices were being displayed about up-and-coming events. Marg and Pete were just as surprised. This was so different from their experience of the more formal occasions they'd attended at churches. Just in front of their seats was an area with toys and books and Freddie asked to get down to play.

Soon the service started. Everything was on the screen, so the service was easy to follow. They looked around to see smiling faces and to hear the volume of singing, realising the church was almost full. People of all ages were participating happily, as though they really meant what they were singing.

Tracey didn't know why she was nervous and used Freddie for an excuse for her attention, but as minutes went by, she found herself increasingly taken up with the singing and the prayers shared. To their surprise, there was then a coffee break before children and young people went out to separate rooms and the adults stayed in the main church. It was Marg who took Freddie for a nappy change and then he trotted with her into the creche. One of the helpers immediately took his attention and Marg slipped away.

Marg, Pete, Max and Tracey were totally engaged in the talk from Ed and the slides he showed to illustrate what he was saying for the next fifteen minutes. Then the service ended and it was time to fetch Freddie. At first Max couldn't find him and he started to panic, but then heard Freddie's laugh. He was in the corner dressing up with one of the helpers, surrounded by hats and wigs and all sorts of costumes. He watched in amazement before going over to Freddie. "Freddie's gorgeous! Will you come again, Freddie?" asked the helper.

"See you soon!" he replied.

"Come and have lunch with us!" Marg urged Tracey. "Well, if you're sure?", Tracey hastily replied, only concerned not to sound too keen. Freddie fell asleep in the car, so Pete lifted him and put him in his cot as soon as they arrived home, while Max put on the kettle and Marg checked the joint in the oven. Tracey arrived. At first, they were all quiet, seemingly not wanting to waken Freddie, but really because they all had so much in their heads and on their hearts.

It was Pete who spoke first. "I've never heard anything like it. What Ed was saying about, what was it? Max got out his mobile and googled the reference Philippians 4:6-7:

"Do not be anxious about anything, but in everything by prayer and supplication with thanksgiving let your requests be made known to God. And the peace of God, which surpasses all understanding, will guard your hearts and your minds in Christ Jesus".

"I actually believe those words. Your Mum and I have, well, I didn't realise it as such, but we've been kind of praying for so long for you and Lisa and Freddie and Tracey and us, without really understanding. What do you say, Marg?"

Marg's eyes filled. "I felt such an overwhelming sense of, I don't know, God's love for us?" It was Tracey who found herself crying "Yes, so did I!"

After several minutes, Max said "You know what I think? Let's invite Ed round for a meal one evening and we can talk with him and ask questions". They all agreed. Without delay, Max left a message on Ed's voicemail. Freddie woke from his nap and after lunch they took him for a walk. At first Tracey was walking with Marg, but then she fell in step with Max who was pushing the buggy. He put his arm round her and said, "Whatever is happening, I feel we're all meant to be together!"

He means as friends, but I want it to be more than that, she longingly thought, before feeling ashamed. She reminded herself it was such early days since Lisa had died.

Ed returned the call and sounded genuinely pleased to be invited round the following Saturday. It was a busy week in the salon, so Tracey didn't have the opportunity to spend time with Max and the family. She felt nervous driving over, not knowing what to expect, but she'd taken extra care to wear something dressier than jeans. "Oh, you look lovely!" Max exclaimed and then he dashed upstairs, only to come down a few minutes later changed from jeans and a T-shirt to trousers and a shirt. Tracey had never seen him look so dressed up. Unobserved, Marg and Pete exchanged glances, but the doorbell rang before anything more was said.

The evening was delightful and there was hardly a break in the conversation, as all four asked Ed questions about the readings and sermon. "Can we come to church tomorrow?" Max asked, looking round at his parents and Tracey.

"Of course!" Ed replied. "In fact, it's a special service, because a family is being baptised". Ed explained that was another word for christening, but the full meaning would become apparent, as they weren't to know that there was a baptistry in the church under the platform, so people could have a full immersion, rather than just a sprinkling of water.

Marg, Pete, Max and Tracey were astonished to hear how the service would start with this baptism, and they were all full of anticipation. Ed explained how baptism was an outward sign of an inward reality of turning away from an old life and welcoming Jesus into a new life. Nothing could prepare them for a husband and wife climbing down into the water, where Ed and another person spoke special words of faith, which the couple affirmed. Then the couple were submerged under the water, and brought up again, to represent Jesus' death and subsequent resurrection. To their surprise, someone they presumed was a grandparent then handed the couple a baby, who was baptised by sprinkling with the same water. After this the family went to change into dry clothes, as the service proceeded and the roof was nearly raised by the singing. Freddie was pleased to go into the crèche, then fell asleep on the way home.

Tracey joined Marg, Pete and Max for lunch again. The conversation was warm but superficial, as each of them seemed lost in processing their own thoughts. It was Tracey who dared to say, "I don't know what's come over me, but I want to tell you how much I love you all and of course Freddie, and it feels all mixed up with this sense of love I feel in that church!" Max, Marg and Pete looked at Tracey, at each other and before they knew it, they were all smiling and laughing, saying they all felt the same and about loving her.

"Why don't you take Freddie out for some fresh air after lunch?" suggested Marg. "Your Dad and I have a few things we need to sort out without Freddie's assistance!"

The sky was looking heavy, but the three took the opportunity to walk before they had to race for cover at the bandstand in the park. It was only a brief shower, so Freddie was delighted that the swings and slides were hardly wet. Tracey exclaimed, "Look at the rainbow!". "Wow, that's beautiful!" Max declared. He then turned to Tracey and continued, "And so are you! I realise it's only early days for me to say this to you, Tracey, but I feel we're meant to be a family together. I intended to wait to ask, but so much is happening that seems important for us all. I love you. Can we get married…I mean, will you marry me?"

Tracey found her hand covering her mouth to suppress a shriek of laughter, before she flung her arms round Max declaring "Yes, let's get married…I really love you too, Max!"

Chapter 4
Retirement and romance

The weeks had passed, and Arthur had been meeting up regularly with Brenda, until she was called by her daughter who needed support with the grandchildren, while her husband was abroad. Arthur decided it was best to put Brenda out of his mind – she may move again, to be nearer her family, if her son in law was going to be working away.

Arthur continued his bus driving, mainly on his favourite Route 52. He had come to know new faces of students travelling to school. Jean and John didn't return to their weekly trip to town after losing Jenny. Arthur still compiled stories in his head about his passengers. He often saw Freddie and Marg, sometimes with Tracey and was so delighted to hear the news about Tracey and Max getting married. What a wonderful outcome! Arthur realised how much he missed Brenda. He received a text from Renée but just deleted it. It was a right decision to let that relationship go.

One day, when his shift ended, Arthur was greeted by a colleague who laughed handing over a rather posh envelope to him. "Looks like you have an admirer!"

Arthur opened it carefully only to find it was an invitation to Max and Tracey's wedding, to him and Brenda.

Arthur was surprised how pleased and nervous he felt about texting Brenda to let her know. He didn't hear back from her that day or the next. The following day he received a text saying she was back at home and would love to meet up.

To say he felt like he was going on a real date rather than a casual meeting with a friend was an understatement. Arthur chided himself. He imagined Brenda would even tell him she was selling up and returning to be near family. It would make perfect sense. He'd actually been making his own plans. There were to be cuts in the scheduled buses and voluntary redundancies would be considered. Although he loved his job, to his astonishment, Arthur asked himself, why not? He'd never married, been fortunate to work all his life and in his early 60's, had very good health. Why didn't he take the opportunity and make it the chance of a lifetime to travel? He purposefully filled his mind with positive thoughts.

Arthur smiled at himself arriving punctually outside Brenda's home. He was always frustrated with letting down his passengers, when the bus was late due to roadworks or other unforeseen complications along the route.

* * *

Brenda looked lovely in an aquamarine dress, which he couldn't help himself declaring: "That dress colour looks smashing on you!"

"Well, I can't remember the last time I had a compliment like that!" Brenda laughed. They sat down and Arthur pulled out the wedding invitation. Before Brenda said anything, Arthur found himself almost blurting out that he quite understood she may not wish to, or be able to come, but he wanted her to see she was included. "I'd love to come!" she butted in.

"You would? You can?"

"Yes! In fact," Brenda continued, "a lot has happened and I'm sorry I've not been in contact, but I wanted to speak to you when things were clearer."

Arthur braced himself and missed the first part of what Brenda was explaining. "Sorry, please can you say that again?" he asked.

Brenda smiled. "My family are moving this way to be closer to me!"

"Wow, so you're not moving back to them!". Arthur found himself smiling and admitting, "Oh I am so pleased, I've really missed spending time with you."

Brenda clasped her hands on his and they laughed. "So, yes, I'd love to come to the wedding!"

"To be honest, I've been doing some thinking too." Arthur explained his plans. "Oh, how wonderful!" Brenda exclaimed. "My late husband and I always promised ourselves we'd travel when he retired, but time ran out for us…"

"Well, Brenda, how about you come with me for the holiday of a lifetime?"

Brenda's eyes sparkled…

* * *

The next weeks were taken up with Brenda back and forth to help her family, who had managed to sell their house very quickly. They put their belongings into storage and moved in with her, while they found the place to be their next home. Grandchildren were registered with new schools and, meanwhile, Arthur's pre-retirement weeks were full of form-filling and his final farewell. It wasn't a big 'do', but nevertheless, to his surprise, a get-together was planned, and he invited Brenda as his plus-one. There was great mirth when those gathered heard they'd met on Route 52, and a bit of competing as to who'd like to be rostered on that route next!

Arthur and Brenda met up with Max, Tracey, Freddie, Marg and Pete, inviting them round to Brenda's, to meet her family. Freddie was in his element with children a few years older than himself and Arthur couldn't believe how he was suddenly amidst so many close friends, after decades spent largely on his own.

Max and Tracey insisted all Brenda's family came to the wedding too. But there was a further surprise when Tracey and Max handed Brenda and Arthur another invitation. They opened the envelope and read the words carefully, looking up for a further explanation.

"Yes, we're all getting baptised the week before the wedding!" Marg and Pete took Arthur and Brenda's hands and told them all that had happened. "We agreed with Max and Tracey that it would be the perfect start to their married life together…and to ours at this stage too!" Arthur and Brenda couldn't believe it. They'd never been to a baptism by immersion before and heard that Freddie would be sprinkled with water too.

* * *

The day arrived and they all met at church, where Ed greeted them. For the first time they met Ed's wife, Marie, but not before Brenda's grandchildren had rushed over to their children, knowing them already from school.

Arthur and Brenda were astonished by the whole experience, never having been 'church people' themselves. In fact, Brenda hadn't even been in a church since her daughter was married, so she had mixed feelings. But they were soon overtaken by the happiness of everyone gathered and the meaningful words of the service.

Arthur had found himself increasingly excited. He had so much to look forward to, but in his heart, there was something else that would make life perfect. He and Brenda had already put down deposits on their cruise. Yes, their plans had really taken shape. They realised they'd both always fancied a cruise as a great means of visiting so many places without the hassle of driving or flying. But with his first redundancy money, Arthur went shopping. He knew Brenda's 55th birthday was coming up. He bought a beautiful aquamarine ring, just as a present to match that beautiful dress. Brenda's daughter had 'borrowed' a ring from Brenda's jewellery box, so Arthur could take it to the jeweller's for sizing up, and then it was returned without her knowledge.

Max and Tracey's wedding day arrived. Arthur really enjoyed driving a minibus he'd hired to take Brenda and family, with Freddie to the wedding. Freddie was very happy being with his new friends. Max had asked his father to be his best man. Tracey had asked Marg to walk her down the aisle, explaining that no other friend could mean more to her than Marg.

Arthur and Brenda joined Brenda's family and Freddie in the front rows of the church, which was full of tangible happiness. There was such a feeling of excitement and contentment.

Ed led a lovely service. At the reception, they all danced. Arthur couldn't remember a time he'd had such fun and there was so much laughter. Catching breath, he and Brenda went out into the last of the chilly sunshine. What beautiful grounds! They walked to the bridge and enjoyed the silence, apart from the distant sounds from the hotel. Then they both started speaking together. "What a lovely day!". They found themselves giggling – could you still do that in your 50's and 60's? Arthur's hand could feel the shape of the ring box in his pocket. It was just a birthday gift…but as he looked at Brenda, Arthur realised that from his side, this was far more than friendship. The words of the marriage service had made such an impact on him. Did he dare? What would she say?

"Brenda", Arthur cleared his throat. "I have a present for you for your birthday, after all it is tomorrow". Brenda found herself blushing… nonetheless, she smiled with anticipation. She couldn't see a gift, maybe it was a voucher in his pocket.

"I've never done this before. I want to make this more than a birthday gift, but I don't know what your feelings are for me. I'm going to just say it". So, on the bridge, very romantically as the sun set, he went down on one knee and proposed to Brenda. "Oh, yes, yes, yes!" She exclaimed and tears filled her eyes.

He hugged and kissed her for the first time. "Brenda", Arthur whispered "I have fallen in love with you and I always want us to be together!" He took the ring box from his pocket, opened it and Brenda gasped. Sparkling, the aquamarine ring caught the glint of the water. "Oh, it's beautiful!" Arthur placed it on her finger. "I am so happy!" Brenda hugged Arthur, with tears of joy.

"Shall I change the cruise tickets, so we can share a cabin for what can be our honeymoon?"

"Oh yes!" Brenda said with glee. "My family can carry on living in my house while we're away, giving them time to look for a new home. But wait a minute – what about I sell it to them and what about we buy a house together?"

"That's a wonderful idea! Let's make our home together! Guess what?" Arthur laughed till the tears streamed down his face. "Have you seen the house for sale, next to Marg and

Pete?" With that Brenda burst out laughing, as he went on: "And guess what, it's number 52!"

John tried reading everything he could find to help him understand what had happened to Jean, since losing Jenny. This took him down all sorts of avenues, including articles and books on grief and loss in bereavement:

'The Kübler-Ross model, or the five stages of grief, describes the emotional journey people often experience after a loss or significant change. These stages, while often presented in a linear fashion, are more accurately viewed as a cyclical process with overlapping and repeating experiences. The five stages are denial, anger, bargaining, depression, and acceptance....'

When John tried to speak to Jean, she said she felt too tired to talk about anything. It was as though she was fading away. He tried to interest her in going to places, even back on the No 52 bus route. He tried without success to engage her in all kinds of ways. She wouldn't go to visit the GP. She ate less and less and took no steps to cook or to do the jobs at home that she'd done before.

He was getting exasperated with her and cross with himself, running out of ideas of how to get 'his Jean' back from where she was disappearing.

Then, out of the blue, Amy rang inviting them over to the farm where she was now living with her partner, Matt, and her daughter, Gillian. John didn't know how or when to approach Jean with this. Their son, Phil and his partner, Liz, had been very concerned about the way Jean was becoming mentally and physically frail. They also had received an invitation to the farm and decided it was time to accept this invitation and move forwards. It wasn't helping anyone to harbour resentments and regrets. So, on their next visit they invited Jean and John to go with them. "I don't mind," Jean quietly stated, as she faintly smiled at Phil. "It would be something to see the old place again." John was so amazed but decided to just take it gently, and they all agreed the time for pick-up.

John reminded Jean a week, then a few days ahead and the day before. He quite expected her to back out of the planned visit, but even on the day, she was up and dressed in readiness, taking more care of her appearance than she had done for months. Surprisingly, Jean ate breakfast and then declared: "We must take a Christmas present with us!"

John was astonished. "Yes, of course we must! What do you suggest?"

"We'll have time to go to the shops before Phil and Liz come, if we go soon."

John couldn't believe his ears, or his eyes, as Jean went about getting ready to leave. "You'll be alright, won't you? I wouldn't want you to be too tired…"

Jean turned to him and with a sigh replied "No, I'm fine, I've had a good, long rest…for months."

John was able to park so they could easily reach M&S. Jean walked slowly but determinedly from one section to the other. Instead of just one present, they had a trolley full of gifts for all the family, which were all beautifully presented, so there was no need to wrap them.

John was expecting Jean to collapse once home. It was more than she had managed to do in such a long time, but she just said that after a spot of lunch she'd put her feet up for a half an hour, until it was time to go.

Now it was the time for Phil and Liz to be surprised. When they arrived, Jean had changed into a lovely, cosy winter trouser suit. Because the jacket was loose, it enabled her to put some warm layers underneath.

The drive only took half an hour. At the end of the farm track the house was aglow with Christmas lights and there was smoke coming out of the chimney. "Ah, I'm glad the fire's going!" Jean laughed.

Amy was full of smiles as she welcomed in her aunt and uncle and cousin and partner. "I've been so looking forward to showing you round your old home! Come on, let me take your coat. I think it's warm everywhere!"

Without hesitation, Jean took Amy's arm, and John was about to follow when laughter came from voices and two men arrived in the hall. "Hello Uncle John, we're so glad you could all make it, and let me introduce Matt to you, the man of the house!" John couldn't believe it. His face must have given away his incredulity. Here was their nephew, Richard, apparently the best of friends with his ex-wife's new partner. Matt shook his hand, but there was no opportunity for further comment, as delighted sounds came from another direction when Gillian, Liz and another woman appeared along with a kitten and a puppy. "What have we here?" John smiled. "We've brought Poppy and Pixie to meet you!" Gillian giggled, as the pets scampered around their feet.

"Let's have a drink!" Matt invited and led them into a wonderful sitting room where there was a roaring fire. Richard then said, "Mandy, this is my Uncle John."

"I'm so pleased to meet you! I met Jean upstairs having the grand tour!" she smiled engagingly.

"I'll unload the car", Phil said.

"I'll help!" Gillian declared, "but we must close the door, so Poppy and Pixie don't get out, as it's dark."

"That will be great, thank you!" Phil declared, taking Gillian's hand.

"I'll come too," laughed Liz.

They carried in boxes of parcels. It was then that John turned to find Jean and Amy joining them. He could not believe the glow on Jean's face. "Let's sit by the fire, and what will you drink?" Amy asked.

"A sherry please!"

Screeches of delight followed as the parcels were distributed and opened before they were all led into the dining room, festooned with garlands. "I helped make those!" declared Gillian, "and I've written your place names, so you know where to sit!" She took her great Aunt Jean's hand without being asked and then her great Uncle John's, while the others found their places.

It was a full Christmas meal. Jean managed a little of everything. At the end of the meal, Matt stood and his smile was genuinely warm and generous. "Amy and I are so very pleased you have come to our home - your home, if I may call you Aunt Jean and Uncle John! I know it's been a tough time for you, but I want to assure you we truly want us all to be family. Richard and I actually go back a long way, and my sister, Mandy and Amy have become the best of friends, and we all love Gillian. We thank you so much for all your presents. Ours to you is not so tangible." With that Amy joined him on his feet, and Gillian jumped up and down with delight. "I've kept the secret!" she squealed.

"In six months' time, if all goes well, we'll be introducing you to a new family member!" said Amy. Everybody gleefully shouted congratulations. With that Liz and Phil stood up and laughed hysterically as they declared: "And we join you in this one, but you'll only have to wait four months!" Jean and John clapped their hands over their mouths in amazement, as the two couples came round the table to hug them. "What wonderful, wonderful news for you all!"

At this point, Poppy and Pixie dived into the room to join in the celebration.

Gillian didn't want them to go, but they all decided to get together again on New Year's Eve, when Matt said his family were coming over. Jean was the first to say, "We'd love to come, wouldn't we John?"

"Absolutely!"

Matt added, "If the weather looks worrying, bring an overnight bag – we'll have the rooms ready, and you can help us with feeding the animals."

"I love doing that! I want to be a farmer!" Gillian proudly declared. "This house could be big enough for us all to live in!"

At the door, Amy put her arms round Jean. "It means so much to have you back!" She meant at the Rogers' farm, but Jean responded with more than one meaning, when she murmured, "It's so good to be back..."

On the way home Jean fell asleep with John's arm round her in the back seat. He thought back to Kubler-Ross's final stage of grief. Acceptance. There was more than one way to interpret that. For them, part of the recovery was in the 'acceptance' not only of how things were now, but the acceptance of an invitation which opened up hope and, well, new life.

With each day Jean looked stronger. A light had been lit in her eyes, and John couldn't believe the change. They invited Phil and Liz round for a meal, which Jean cooked, so they could hear their news in detail.

"We wanted to tell you before, but we could see what a toll this year had taken on you with one shock after another. We wanted to be sure this baby was safely on its way first. We want you to be the first to know we're having a girl - and we're going to call her Jenny!"

Tears of joy overwhelmed Jean and John. "We thought you'd decided not to have children?"

Phil looked at Liz and then he explained that losing both his Uncle Giles and Aunt Jenny, and the break-up between Richard and Amy, had really made them think long and hard about what they wanted in life. And now they realised, that included children. When they talked together openly, everything happened very quickly!

"And what about Richard knowing Matt? Do you know what happened? It just seems an unbelievable situation," John asked.

Phil explained what had happened.

"Well, that was just an incredible coincidence! They knew each other through work. One day Matt told Rich he was agonising over having met someone he really wanted to be with, but she was married and she had a child. He felt very strongly about not breaking up marriages and especially families, when people had promised to stay together. They decided to meet at

Matt's farm and have a good chat. You know how we're always told that men find it hard to share their feelings? But Matt did just that. During the evening, Matt's sister popped in. That was Mandy! She was between jobs and helping out on the farm. It was just as though it was meant to be. Mandy sat down with them, and it was only then that Matt explained Mandy knew all about his dilemma, and for the first time said the woman he had fallen for was called 'Amy'. Rich was so taken aback. He thought it couldn't be the same 'Amy', but it was and of course the child was Gillian. Matt was so shocked and desperately sorry. It was then that Rich realised his own feelings for Amy had been changing for longer than he'd admitted to himself and to her. As he listened, Rich sensed that Matt and Amy would be a natural couple to go on together. When Matt went out to check round the farm for the night, Mandy stayed behind with Rich and she was just so understanding. It had been quite a bombshell after all. He thought she was just feeling sorry for him, but it started from there…and the rest as they say is history!"

"I'm so glad that Rich and I are close again. I'd so missed him! You know he's been more like a brother to me than just a cousin."

Jean and John felt that everything was going to turn out right and their granddaughter Gillian was happily in the middle of them all.

* * *

New Year's Eve was a wonderfully happy time as all the families gathered together at the farm. As the clock struck midnight, they all sang together linking arms:

For auld lang syne, my dear,
For auld lang syne,
We'll take a cup of kindness yet,
For auld lang syne.

This New Year's Eve was one when a cup of kindness was overflowing, as Matt's family mingled with Amy's. Jean and John were the same sort of age as Matt's parents and had much in common. Gillian had been in her element, with all her uncles and aunts as well as two lots of parents and grandparents. Far from seeming spoilt, she'd busied herself with her young charges of Poppy and Pixie and with her wellies on, doing the evening check on the farm's animals, accompanied by her great Auntie Jean.

"I know all about how you used to live here. You will come often won't you, so we can do the farm together with Matt and Mummy?"

"Oh yes!" Jean replied, smiling as she pictured her dear sister, Jenny's face, "You won't be able to keep me away!"

"And you can help with the baby!"

Jean turned her face, so Gillian wouldn't see her tears of happiness. Yes, 'new life' was coming with the new year…

Didn't someone once say that life is like a tapestry? As far as we can see, the picture is colourful and beautiful, but turn it over and there are many loose ends, where the embroidery silk has been broken and knots where a section has ended, or just begun...

Just a few people on a bus... Some lives become entwined. Others take another course. We all influence each other, although we may not be fully aware of it. Surprises await all of us along life's journey, whether we're on a bus or not. Friends and family may be found and made in unexpected ways and places.

The familiar rites of passage – birth, baptism, marriage and death - take various forms at different ages and stages, but they are all vitally significant: beginnings, endings and everything in-between.

If we take time to clear the smears on the windows of life, which sometimes stop us really seeing what or who is around us - as well as what is within - we can find faith to make every day count...

Printed in Dunstable, United Kingdom